His to Command

Opal Carew

St. Martin's Griffin

New York

HIS TO COMMAND. Copyright © 2013 by Opal Carew. All rights reserved. Printed in the United States of America. For information, address St. Martin's Press, 175 Fifth Avenue, New York, N.Y. 10010.

www.stmartins.com

The following chapters in this book were previously published as individual e-books: *The Chase* copyright © 2013 by Opal Carew; *The Capture* copyright © 2013 by Opal Carew; *The Revelation* copyright © 2013 by Opal Carew; *The Arrangement* copyright © 2013 by Opal Carew; *The Submission* copyright © 2013 by Opal Carew; *The Surrender* copyright © 2013 by Opal Carew.

ISBN 978-0-312-67463-2 (trade paperback)
ISBN 978-1-250-03313-0 (e-book)

St. Martin's Griffin books may be purchased for educational, business, or promotional use. For information on bulk purchases, please contact Macmillan Corporate and Premium Sales Department at 1-800-221-7945 extension 5442 or write specialmarkets@macmillan.com.

10 9 8 7 6 5 4 3 2

To Wes, with affection.

Thirteen is a charm!

His to Command

The Chase

It couldn't be him!

The thought sent involuntary shudders quivering up Kate's spine as she stared out the van window at the disturbingly familiar man calmly reading a magazine less than ten yards away, totally oblivious to her scrutiny. No, surely it wasn't him. Her imagination must be playing tricks. She thought she'd finally recovered from her irrational fear of running into Matt Pearce again. After all, New York City seemed a lifetime ago and that was where she'd left him.

Except that two years wasn't nearly enough time to soothe the pain.

As she continued driving by the main entrance of Cavendish Mall, the large shopping center near her house, moving slowly because of the density of shoppers out for the post-holiday sales, she allowed her gaze to travel the length of him, determined to convince herself that this long, lean stranger, who had the audacity to look like the man she had prayed never to see again, truly was a stranger. He stood with his legs carelessly crossed as he leaned against the brick wall near the entrance.

The day was mild for Connecticut in late December and his overcoat, unbuttoned, was pushed open by the hand he had stuffed in his pants pocket. The clothes visible underneath—expensive and well cut—emphasized his broad shoulders and narrow waist. With his head bent toward the magazine, she couldn't see much of his face, but he had dark, wavy hair, styled with the same flair as Matt's had been.

She watched as a light breeze lifted a few locks and swirled them onto his forehead. Long, careless tanned fingers swept them back. Kate's throat constricted as she remembered running her own fingers through Matt's hair and the feel of the sleek strands against her skin. Thrusting away the disturbing memories, she forced her attention back to the stranger. Unlike Matt's, gray sprinkled through this man's hair, and he was a little thinner.

The sharp blare of a car horn behind her made her jump. She'd been holding up traffic. The man glanced up at the noise and . . .

Oh, my God. Either that was him—or Matt Pearce had an exact double living right here in Connecticut.

Denial flooded through her, overriding the evidence of her own senses. She simply could not believe Matt stood within the sound of her voice. For a fleeting second, his gaze locked with hers. She felt her lungs freeze, as though someone had stolen the last breath of air in existence. Those unforgettable eyes, the exact shade of the sky at midnight, did not belong to a stranger.

As though he moved in slow motion, she watched a slight frown etch his brow, then saw his eyes widen in obvious recognition. The magazine fluttered as his arm dropped to his side and he stepped forward. It would only take him a few steps to reach the van. A choking panic welled within her as her fingers clenched impossibly tight around the steering wheel. She couldn't seem to force her rigid body to take action, even though he continued to move toward her. The driver behind her honked again, shattering the frozen shell of dread that held her immobile. She pressed the accelerator, lurching the van into motion.

Had that been anger chasing the recognition from his eyes?

Kate parked the van in her friend Ellen's parking space at the back of the apartment building. What would Matt be doing at a shopping mall? Of course, she remembered when his sister and young niece had come to visit him in New York and he'd gone shopping with them for souvenirs. Maybe he was buying something for little Lizzie. Or maybe one of his high-tech gizmos was being launched and he wanted to see how the major department store was handling it. He was very hands-on in that way.

She pushed thoughts of Matt out of her mind as she set about the task of getting her new rocking chair upstairs. It would never have fit in her own little car, so Ellen had lent her the van to pick it up, along with a trolley. She wrestled the new rocker through the lobby and up the elevator. Once she had it unpacked, she called Ellen to come and see it.

Kate set out some refreshments, then slumped into the chair to await the arrival of her friend. Unfortunately, with the cessation of activity, her thoughts again turned to the man she'd seen at Cavendish Mall.

Matt.

Had it really been him?

The jolt she'd felt as their gazes had locked sent remembered sparks crackling across her nerve endings. Surely, she'd only imagined the flare of recognition in his eyes. Certainly, there'd been an uncanny similarity between this man's appearance and Matt's unforgettable features, but that didn't mean they were one and the same person. Besides, why would he be here in Connecticut? He was the owner of a large computer firm and . . .

She shifted uncomfortably in her chair as the names of several high-tech corporations that had their headquarters in the area sprang unbidden to her mind. Had Matt's company set up an office here, too?

She continued to rock, trying to shake some sense into her brain. She was being silly. This speculation was all based on the possibility that the man she'd seen today was Matt, and it probably hadn't been. The anniversary of when she'd moved here was coming up and that reminded her of the turmoil her life had been in when she'd left New York City two years ago. Her relationship with Matt had fallen apart shortly before that, then things had gone from bad to worse and she'd had to sell the wonderful apartment she'd finally managed to put a down payment on. She'd loved that place, and she'd loved living in the city. But she'd had no choice other than to leave.

No, surely her overactive imagination had tricked her into thinking that was Matt today.

Matt Pearce was definitely not in Connecticut.

A knock sounded on the door and she strode across the room to answer it, relieved for a distraction from her turbulent emotions.

"Oh, it's lovely. Can I sit in it?" Ellen exclaimed when she saw the rocking chair.

The chair was a golden oak glider with beige-striped upholstery and a matching ottoman. She'd been torn between the beige and the berry red, but beige had won out.

"Be my guest." Kate made a sweeping gesture toward the chair and smiled as Ellen sank reverently into it, stroking the beige fabric over the armrests.

"I love it," Ellen said.

Kate sliced her famous blueberry-lemon pound cake— famous because it was the only thing she could bake— and handed Ellen a serving.

"So . . . ," Ellen said, letting the word linger. "A handsome man was asking about you this afternoon. He saw you driving my van."

Apprehension jolted through Kate like a major electrical shock. Her fork slipped from her suddenly numb fingers and clattered onto her plate.

"What?"

Ellen put down her fork and leaned forward, concern sharpening her intent stare.

"Kate, what the heck's the matter?"

"Who was he? Have you ever seen him before?" Amazingly, her voice sounded steady, totally unaffected by the tendrils of dread coiling through her. *God, please, don't let it be Matt.*

"Sure I have. I don't go around talking to strangers, you know. I met him when he moved in a few weeks ago."

"Moved in?" Kate's voice tightened, vibrating with tension. This couldn't be happening. Was Matt Pearce living in this building?

Ellen plunked her plate onto her knees and grasped one of Kate's shaking hands in her own. "Calm down. I promise I won't tell him who you are if you don't want me to. That's why I brought it up. I think he wants me to introduce you so he can ask you for a date."

"A date?" Kate shook her head. "Oh, no, I don't think that's a good idea." If it was Matt, she didn't know why he would be looking for her, but it wouldn't be for a date.

"At least give him a chance. He's young, very attactive—"

"Ellen, I don't think—"

"—and a doctor. He's just getting started in his practice but—"

"He's a what?"

"A doctor. What is the matter with you?"

A doctor.

Matt was definitely not a doctor. He owned Cutting Edge Industries, a major high-tech firm.

"What did he look like?"

Ellen smiled. "Definitely handsome. He's tall, obviously works out, has sandy hair. And big brown eyes you could get lost in."

A definite catch.

Kate felt as though a devastating weight had been heaved from her chest. With her renewed ability to breathe in a normal fashion, she inhaled deeply, and started to feel almost lightheaded. She broke out laughing.

"What is the matter with you?" Ellen demanded.

Kate covered her mouth with her hand, quieting her frantic laughter, and took a few more deep breaths.

"I'm sorry. I'm just in a strange mood today."

Ellen studied her uncertainly. "So, should I discourage Chris next time he asks? I just thought you might like to ask him to be your date for our New Year's Eve party."

Chris. Not Matt.

Kate stifled another giggle. She almost felt compelled to accept Ellen's attempt at matchmaking to make up for her unprecedented behavior—but she really didn't want to be fixed up with someone. She shifted in her chair, preparing to disappoint Ellen yet again.

"You know, I'm really not ready—"

Ellen waved her hand. "Yeah, I know. I've heard it before. You know, the way you're acting, you'd think I was trying to push you into an arranged marriage rather than a simple date," she teased.

"I'm sorry, Ellen." Kate set her cup down on the coffee table, pushing aside the disturbing memory. "I really appreciate your concern, but—"

"It's okay. I understand. I need to learn not to be so pushy." Ellen grabbed a cup from the tray on the table. "Now, how about a cup of coffee?"

After Ellen had gone, Kate tidied up the dishes and climbed into bed. Still a bit wobbly from the shock of believing Matt was on her tail, she forced herself to calm down and tried to drive him out of her thoughts. Even if the man she'd seen had been Matt, why would he want to hunt her down? Maybe he'd wanted to possess her two years ago—completely and with a frightening obsession—but surely after all this time, he no longer cared.

That night, as she lay in bed, Kate couldn't stop thinking about Matt. When she'd met him, he'd swept her off her feet. Handsome, powerful, charismatic. He'd had it all. And his potent masculinity had awed her.

She remembered their third date. The scent of fresh-cut gardenias in a glass vase on the table. Candles. Moonlight. The table set on his large balcony overlooking the city.

Matt, dazzlingly attractive, sitting beside her, enfolding her trembling hand in the warmth of his, pressing his lips to her palm, devastating her senses. She'd noticed a startling intensity in his unwavering blue eyes as if she were the most fascinating person he'd ever met, but he'd hesitated, as if uncertain. Until that moment, Matt Pearce—savvy executive, master of every situation—had never been uncertain. Yet, he'd parted his lips as if to say something, but then changed his mind. She'd wondered what he'd intended to say, but then he'd brushed his lips against her temple and electricity had shimmered through her.

She sighed and rolled onto her side.

God, and the first time they'd had sex, she'd nearly fainted with need. He'd been so . . . dominating.

They'd been out several times, and he'd been a perfect gentleman, but the good-night kisses were becoming more heated, and it had been clear they'd both wanted more. She'd also sensed he'd been holding back, which was a good thing, because when she experienced how intense being with him could be, it had unnerved her.

But it had been intensely sexy.

She closed her eyes and drifted back to that first time. She'd invited him in for coffee, but he'd pulled her into his arms as soon as the door closed behind them. His heated kisses had thrilled her and she'd wanted him more than she'd ever wanted any man before.

"Do you like a strong, powerful man, Kate?"

He was so close, so masculine. His breath wafted against her ear and she felt faint with desire.

"Yes," she whispered.

He tightened his arm around her waist, pulling her snug against his body. Her nipples hardened, thrusting against the lace of her bra.

"Do you want me to touch you, Kate? To strip off your clothes and touch your breasts?"

Her insides quivered at his masterful intensity, and his eyes held her mesmerized.

"To lick your hard nipples? To suck them into my mouth?" he asked.

She sucked in air, inhaling the spicy, male scent of him, desperately wanting him to do all those things.

"Do you want me to be soft and gentle?" He nibbled the base of her neck, sending electricity jolting through her. "Or would you like me to back you up against this wall and take you now, hard and fast?"

She could feel his erection against her hip. Thick and hard. Longer than she'd ever imagined. Her insides clenched in need. She wanted to feel it inside her.

Kate lay panting and tried to shake the memories from her mind. Damn, now she was frustrated, and longing for him in her bed. Damn Matt for showing up and stirring these feelings in her. Every time he came into her life, even at a distance like now, it messed her up. The sex with him had been mind-blowing, but she had been shocked and surprised at her own behavior. Her will had melted away at his authoritative words, until finally she had begged him to take her. To control her. Her willingness to become completely submissive to him had unnerved her. She had never behaved that way before.

She never would have thought she'd allow a man to dominate her. To *want* a man to dominate her. But she had. With him.

The extent of her submission, of her willingness to beg and to give over complete control to him, had disturbed her deeply. What did that say about her?

A chill quivered through her. Then she'd found out just how disastrous it was to trust a man like Matt Pearce.

Gripped by claustrophobia as swarms of people pressed by her, Kate zigzagged through the crowd of busy shoppers at Cavendish Mall. After her conversation with Ellen last week, Kate had wondered whether she really should rethink her social situation. It was the start of a new year—a good time to embrace some changes. To try and find some happiness. Loosening up and taking some time away from work would be a good start. She'd even thought about giving the handsome doctor Ellen had told her about a chance, but ultimately she had turned down Ellen's suggestion of inviting him to her New Year's Eve party because she wasn't quite ready.

Ever since she'd started her own company, all she seemed to do was work 24-7, which allowed very little opportunity to meet people. Plus, about two months ago, her business partner had informed her he'd been offered a great job in Los Angeles and he wanted to exercise the clause in their partnership contract to have her buy him out. The problem was, unfortunately, they were only starting to see a profit and she didn't have the kind of money she needed to pay what was required. So she was in search of an investor, and until that was sorted out, her personal life would have to stay on hold.

She climbed aboard the crowded escalator, heading to the third floor. A few moments later, she stepped toward a stylish shop with several female mannequins dressed in formfitting business suits.

Walking inside was like leaving a raging river to step onto a quiet shore. The thick carpet cushioned her feet, a welcome relief from the marble flooring outside, and soft, peaceful music drifted around her, soothing the rapid rhythm of her heart.

The elegant, wood-framed mirrors, smoked-glass tables, and cushioned chairs told Kate this was not the kind of store she was used to shopping in. She didn't let that intimidate her, however. If she was going to meet with potential investors, she needed to look confident, in control, and successful. Her budget was tight right now, but this was a necessity . . . and the suits were on sale this week.

She meandered past racks of blouses and dresses and

made her way to the back of the store. She glanced through the racks until she found some gray suits. Several sizes hung lifelessly on the hangers. She riffled through the selection and, finding one in her size, pulled it from the rack.

"May I help you, madam?"

Kate glanced around to see a tall woman, impeccably dressed in a tailored black suit with a white silk blouse, watching her.

"Yes, I'd like to try this on."

The woman smiled and took the hanger, then led Kate to a changing room. She hung the suit in the small room and stepped aside. "Would you like me to bring a few more selections? We have a very nice royal blue that would go fabulous with your lovely auburn hair."

"No, thank you." Kate didn't want to wear anything that bright. "Maybe something in charcoal, though."

"I could bring some blouses, too."

Kate nodded, then closed the door of the changing room. She enjoyed the next half hour of being pampered and persuaded to splurge. The saleswoman, generous with her flattery, regaled Kate with compliments about how the fitted jacket accentuated her lithe figure and how the slit over the right leg added a hint of the seductive without being too daring. Kate clung desperately to common sense while the woman suggested a beautiful silk blouse to go with the suit, along with a delicious assortment of lacy lingerie to wear underneath.

The blouse was gorgeous, but she had several good, serviceable blouses at home. Pretty lingerie, however, was a different story.

At first, she refused to try any on, until a pretty red and black lace bustier and matching thong caught her eye. She couldn't resist trying them on. As she studied herself in the mirror—her breasts hiked up high, her long legs bare, the bustier making her body look shapely and sexy—she couldn't help thinking of Matt. He would love this on her. She could just imagine his blue eyes darkening as he gazed at her.

Heat washed through her. And she would love him taking the lingerie off her.

Oh, God, what was she thinking? Matt wasn't in her life anymore, and for good reason. If she saw him again, she would avoid him. She did *not* want to see him again. She did not want to talk to him. The man was dangerous.

She changed into her own clothes again and left the changing room. The saleswoman already had her new purchase in a suit bag hanging behind the counter. Kate looked at the black and red lingerie on the hanger in her hand and waffled for a moment, then drew in a deep breath and laid it on the counter.

"This, too." She pulled her credit card from her purse.

Matt Pearce wasn't the only man in the world. She deserved to have something sexy and feminine to wear, just for herself. And who knew? Maybe things would work out between her and that handsome doctor.

"Would you like a pair of black stockings to go with those?" the saleslady asked.

Kate nodded. Why not?

Once the transaction was complete, the saleslady handed her the suit bag, which Kate draped over her arm, and a small black and gray paisley bag with her new undergarments and stockings.

She returned to the flow of intent shoppers, beaming with thoughts of the possibility of meeting a new man. Going out to dinner, maybe seeing a show. After she got things sorted out with her company, she would make a point of ensuring she took time for a social life, and going out and having some fun. And definitely finding a man she could show off this new lingerie to.

With a big smile on her face, she stepped onto the escalator, descending to the second floor where she would slip into the department store at the center of the mall to treat herself to a new nail polish.

"Kate!"

Her breath caught in her throat. That voice!

She swung around and saw what she feared most.

Matt Pearce, staring directly at her. He leaned over the third-floor railing overlooking the escalator, only three yards away—straight up.

She gasped and glanced desperately at the press of people in front of her. Panic exploded through her. She pushed past the teenage couple in front of her, excusing herself, then continued past the next few people, ignoring the dirty looks she received along the way. Mutters of discontent behind her made it clear Matt had decided to pursue her. At the bottom of the second floor, she hopped off the escalator and slipped into the throngs of people.

"Kate. Wait!"

He was much too close. Kate hazarded a glance over her shoulder and saw Matt only several yards behind her. His height made him visible over the crowd. Dodging back and forth amid the clumps of people, she headed toward the center of the floor. Would she be able to duck into one of the service hallways, under the obscurity of the crowd? Matt would assume she'd head for the set of stairs and continue that way once he lost sight of her.

Before she could swing around the corner, she felt a tug on her arm. She yelped and stumbled. The bag with her lingerie had caught on an information display as she'd rushed past. A quick yank didn't free it and a quick glance back told her she didn't have time to struggle with it, so reluctantly, she let go and forged ahead.

"Kate!"

She actually thought he had reached her when she felt a hand brush against her arm through the sea of people as she surged forward. But it hadn't been Matt. The mirrors on a nearby wall showed that someone had tried to grab her attention, holding up her precious paisley bag. But Kate couldn't stop. Matt was closing the distance rapidly.

Suddenly, through the throng, she could see that the mirrors surrounded an elevator only a few steps in front of her. And the doors were closing. She sucked in a lungful of air and raced forward. She made it inside but she'd caused the doors to whoosh open again. Glancing back, she saw Matt burst through the crowd. She jabbed the CLOSE DOOR button.

As though in slow motion, the next moment stretched on forever. Completely helpless, her breathing stopped and every part of her body froze while the opening between the doors shrank as Matt raced toward it. With his arm flung out in front of him, he strained to reach the barrier before it closed between them. Kate's throat tightened. Anxiety ripped through her at the thought of being trapped in the tiny elevator with no possible escape.

Face-to-face with Matt.

Her heart thumped loudly as the doors finally closed. The elevator began to move downward.

Panting, Kate leaned against the wall, the rasping sound intensely loud in the silent elevator. The other shoppers made a concerted effort to ignore her and she edged toward the doors, ready to flee once they parted.

Until this moment, she'd always hated the layout of this mall. The stairs and escalators were placed at each end of the single straight corridor, while the elevator she rode was in the center. She knew Matt couldn't dodge his way to a set of stairs and get back in time to catch her, especially through the crowd of Saturday shoppers.

The doors whooshed open and she dashed through the crowd and out the mall's main door. Within moments, she had reached her car, unlocked it, and hopped inside. As she started the ignition, she had trouble controlling her breathing as she gulped in the frigid January air. As she pulled into the main traffic area of the parking lot, she gasped as she glanced in her rearview mirror and saw Matt tear out the main entrance, scanning the parking lot with an efficient eye. A line of tightly packed traffic in front of her prevented her escape, and she was confined between a concrete pillar and a narrow walkway.

Trapped.

Her heart thundered in her chest. Any second now

he'd recognize her car and there'd be no escape. But then Matt marched past the cars behind her and into the parking area.

Not toward her.

The car in front of her started to move. She pressed the accelerator, moving slowly ahead with the traffic. She watched in her side mirror as Matt walked toward a gray van and glanced inside. She giggled nervously as realization struck. Last week, he had seen her driving Ellen's van. She sucked in a deep breath and released it slowly.

He thought she drove a van.

Five minutes later, she drove onto the highway and sped away from the mall.

If she'd thought it would help, she'd have gone faster.

She frowned. Matt knew she was a creature of habit, and typically went out shopping every Saturday around the same time. She wasn't sure why he had been at the mall last week, but she was sure this week it was because he'd been watching for her.

But why?

When Kate arrived at her apartment, she heard the phone ringing. She unlocked the door and rushed inside to snatch up the handset.

"Kate, thank goodness you're home." Ellen's voice on the other end, out of breath, almost frantic, accelerated Kate's heartbeat. Her fingers flexed tightly around the phone.

"What's wrong, Ellen?"

"You're asking *me* what's wrong? For heaven's sake, I saw you racing through Cavendish Mall with that guy right behind you. What the heck was going on?"

She struggled for something to say that would satisfy her friend, but failed miserably. She pressed her hand to her forehead and shoved her hair back. "Ellen, it was nothing."

"I don't believe you. Look, I'll be right over and we'll talk. It'll take a few minutes because I'm just leaving the mall now. Is there anything you want me to tell mall security about him?"

"About who?" Kate asked, afraid of Ellen's answer.

"The guy who was after you, who else? Come on, Kate. Get with it."

Kate sank onto a dining room chair. "Why would security—"

"Are you kidding? When I saw you in trouble, I raced straight to get help."

Oh, God, Ellen hadn't really reported Matt, had she? Images of Matt being handcuffed and dragged off to jail flared in Kate's mind.

"Did they . . . go after him?"

"No, mall security isn't what it's cracked up to be. I was a few minutes from calling the real police. If you hadn't picked up . . ." She heard her friend take a deep calming breath.

It was just as well. Even if the police had apprehended Matt, he would have had them apologizing profusely for detaining him, and probably offering to help find her. He had a knack for turning every situation to his own advantage.

"Do you know this guy?" Ellen asked.

"Ellen, I just . . . really don't want to talk about this."

"Okay, not over the phone." Ellen's frustration was clear.

Kate could imagine her friend's face puckered into a scowl.

"But I'm coming over there right now so we can talk in person," Ellen continued.

By the time Ellen rapped on Kate's door, she'd pulled together a pot of coffee and a plate of chocolate chip cookies, desperate to distract herself from agitated thoughts of Matt.

"So," Ellen said as she strode into the room, "tell me what that was all about. Who was that guy?"

Kate waved her to a chair and sat across from her. She poured some coffee for both of them from the thermal jug she'd set on the table, then added cream and sugar to her own cup. Ellen sipped her black coffee, watching Kate carefully.

"Remember I told you that just before I moved here, I was in a relationship, but it didn't work out?"

That's all she'd told Ellen about it. Just the bare facts.

"Sure. That's why you never date. I figured you're still hung up on the guy."

More like gun-shy, but Kate didn't confirm or deny Ellen's assumption.

When Kate didn't explain any more, Ellen's eyes widened in astonishment. "You mean that was him?"

At Kate's confirming nod, Ellen's expression of astonishment shifted to one of anger. She grabbed the phone from the stand and handed it to Kate. "Call the police," she commanded. "Right now."

Kate took the phone and laid it on the table. "I'm not going to do that."

Ellen sighed in exasperation. "You're crazy. The man could be dangerous."

"Ellen, I am not going to call the police."

"But the way he was chasing you, I don't think he had a pleasant chat in mind." Ellen examined Kate's expression. "Have you seen him hanging around recently?"

Kate pursed her lips. "It doesn't matter."

"Uh-huh. The guy's stalking you." Then sympathy filled her eyes and her tone softened. "Kate, you really need to call the police."

Kate's sense of helplessness flashed to annoyance.

"Why would I? They aren't going to do anything just because an ex-boyfriend pursued me in a mall. And even if they did, Matt is a rich and powerful man. With his resources, he'd be out immediately." A pounding started in her temples and she pressed her palm against her forehead.

Ellen paused, watching her with concern.

"I know I get a little overzealous sometimes, but . . ." She reached out and took Kate's hand. "I'm just worried about you."

Kate patted their clasped fingers. "I know. Look, I'm sure he just wanted to talk."

"If you think that, why did you run?"

Kate frowned as her gaze darted to Ellen. What could she possibly say?

"Kate, why don't you tell me about what happened? For instance, why did you break up with the guy?"

Kate's hands clenched tightly around her mug as she shook her head.

"Just go back to the beginning and tell me as much as you're comfortable with," Ellen said gently. "From the look of you, you really need to talk about it."

Kate stared into her coffee, wondering if she should. It couldn't hurt if she was cautious. She took a quick sip of coffee, giving herself time to compose her thoughts, then she placed her mug on the table.

"All right."

Ellen leaned forward in her chair and nodded. Kate could feel her friend scrutinizing her every movement, which made her more nervous.

"I was the project leader for a consulting contract for Matt's company. That's how I met him."

"You weren't worried about an office romance?"

"Not really. I didn't actually work for him. I was a contractor and didn't even work on-site. The only reason we met was because he visited our offices to meet my team. Later, I went to his office to talk to some of his staff, and Matt happened by. He invited me to lunch, and things progressed from there."

A half smile turned up her lips as she remembered the flutter of her heart when he'd asked her to lunch and she'd sensed his interest had more to do with her than the project. "He was this incredibly sexy, intelligent, successful hunk and I just couldn't believe he was interested in me."

"Come on, Kate. Have you been near a mirror lately?"

Self-consciously, Kate shoved her hair behind her ears and stroked its length. Matt had always loved her long, auburn hair.

"I know there were things about me he found attractive but . . . Well, every time he stared at me with that sexy grin on his face, I had to stop myself from glancing around to see who he was really looking at."

Ellen waved a cookie in Kate's direction. "You obviously had something that attracted him or he wouldn't still be chasing you after all this time."

Kate sipped her coffee. How had such a wonderful beginning led her to such heartache?

"Did you love him?"

The unexpected question caught her off guard. She stared at the arrangement of pink silk roses on the center of the table. She didn't have to think about the answer. She thought about it every night before she went to sleep and every morning after she woke up. Her dreams wouldn't let her forget. Nights full of passion, and pain.

"Yes, I loved him."

"So why did you break it off?"

Oh, damn, she couldn't answer that. At least, not the whole reason. She tightened her fingers around the mug, refusing to think about the nightmare that had torn her from Matt.

She grabbed a cookie and nibbled. Maybe it would be good for her to tell Ellen part of it. To share what she'd never shared with anyone before.

"I . . ." Her free hand bunched into a fist. This was hard. She set the cookie down. "When I was with Matt, I didn't like how I behaved."

Ellen's eyebrows raised, but she said nothing.

"Matt was always strong-willed and when we were . . . together . . ." She glanced at Ellen. "He was very dominating."

Ellen's eyes narrowed. "So, in the bedroom he was too rough with you?"

"No, not that. It's not the way he was, it's the way I reacted to him."

At Kate's hesitation, Ellen shook her head. "I'm not quite getting it."

"I became another woman. He took command, and I *wanted* him to. I wanted him to totally control me." She drew in a deep breath. "And that bothered me."

"Really? Because there's nothing wrong with a little role-playing in the bedroom . . . as long as he didn't take things too far."

He *had* gone too far, but that's not what Kate wanted to talk about.

"But to totally submit to a man? It didn't feel right."

"They why did you allow it?"

Kate shook her head. "It's not that I allowed it. As I said, I wanted it. I *needed* it." She stood up and paced. "The closer we got, the more I gave up to him. I felt I was losing myself."

"Did he take advantage of your submission? Pressure you to do things you didn't want to do?"

A memory flashed through her mind. Of lying in bed, Matt stroking her cheek with a loving look in his eyes.

"No, never." Her jaw clenched. But that wasn't really true. At the end, during that party . . .

"Kate, are you okay?"

She drew in another deep breath. "Of course." She gazed at Ellen. "It wasn't about what Matt did."

Again, that wasn't quite true. Ultimately, it had been what Matt did that caused her to walk away, but even before that, Kate had struggled with the relationship, and still didn't understand why she'd behaved the way she had.

"It's about why I submitted to him so completely."

"And why is that?" Ellen asked.

"That's the thing. I really don't understand it."

"Well, okay. Tell me a bit about your childhood."

Kate thought back. She really didn't like thinking about her childhood. She'd been happy to get out on her own and away from her family.

"Well, my father was overbearing. And very critical."

For as long as she could remember, he had constantly berated her mother. Then as Kate and her brother got older, he'd started on them, too. He'd often told Kate she would never amount to anything, and she was sure that had led to a lack of trust in her own abilities. Something she'd had to fight against her whole life, including getting through college. She'd had to keep telling herself she could do it and not let his constant voice in her head discourage her.

"My mother never really stood up to him," Kate continued.

Her mother hadn't protected Kate and her brother from the emotional abuse. As an adult, Kate realized her mother had been incapable of doing so, but as a child, Kate had felt that lack of protection as a deep betrayal.

Neither of her parents had been a very good role model, and Kate had certainly learned not to trust authority figures, even when they meant well, like her mother had.

A big reason Kate had been attracted to Matt was because while he was authoritative, he was slow to anger, he stood up for what he believed, and he encouraged his subordinates to grow and thrive.

"It sounds like you don't want to be overwhelmed by a domineering man, because from your mother's example you're afraid it makes you weak. And you said your father was critical of you. Was Matt critical of you?"

Kate gazed at her. "No. He was actually very encouraging."

"So, although he dominated you, he was nothing like your father." Ellen squeezed Kate's hand. "You know, maybe you should talk to him and try to work out your issues. You said you still loved the guy." She shrugged.

"Maybe you could still make it work. I mean, he *is* gorgeous." She winked. "And you said he's rich. He's certainly worth a little effort. Maybe you can convince yourself that it's okay being submissive—which it is, as long as it's only in the bedroom—or learn to be the one who takes charge. Who knows? He might just love it."

Ellen's total about-face flummoxed Kate. "A minute ago, you were telling me to call the police on the guy. What gives?"

"Well, honey, that was before I realized you were running from yourself, not him."

That night, Kate replayed the conversation with Ellen in her head. It had been good talking to her about her relationship with Matt. She'd never told anyone how she reacted to Matt, and Ellen's acceptance of it, even encouragement, helped.

But Ellen was wrong about Kate being able to make it work. Kate had thought about that a lot during the lonely nights after she'd walked away. Even if things hadn't turned out so terribly wrong, she didn't believe the two of them could ever have made it work.

When they'd still been together, she had tried to change how she reacted to him. Even tried to take control. It hadn't turned out as she'd expected.

A few months into the relationship, Kate had been feeling a little overwhelmed by her submissiveness. How could any woman in this day and age allow herself to be controlled by a man? Especially after women had fought for so long to have control in a man's world. She'd felt like a traitor to womankind.

Yet, she'd loved being with Matt. When she realized she was falling in love with him, she'd decided it was time to do something about it and try something new.

It had been on a Saturday afternoon, and she'd been spending the weekend with him at a luxurious country house he'd rented. He'd had a few hours of work to do that day, so he'd been in the den at the computer, while she'd been out by the pool.

As she lay stretched out on the lounge chair, she imagined Matt sitting beside her, wearing only a bathing suit, his muscular chest and well-sculpted abs on display. She'd love to convince him to go skinny-dipping with her. The thought of him stripping off his swimming trunks and walking to the pool with the hot afternoon sun blazing on his naked body as his large cock swung back and forth set her insides quivering. He'd dive into the water and surface, his body glazed in glistening water. Then he'd walk toward her and . . . things would progress nicely from there.

She sighed, an image of his big, hard cock in her mind. She licked her lips, wishing she could wrap her hands around it right now. Wishing she could take it in her mouth.

Then she realized there was nothing stopping her. He was only a few yards away, with only a brick wall between them. She could march in the patio door and down the hall in ten seconds flat. *The fact that he was working and she'd have to coax him away made her realize this was a great way to turn the tables. Give her a chance to be in control.*

She put her book on the teak table beside the lounge chair and stood up. Then a grin curled her lips. It would be much easier to distract him from his work if she was naked. She reached behind her and unfastened her bikini top, then wiggled her bottoms down her legs and off. As she walked toward the patio door, she cupped her right breast, and grazed her thumb tip over the nipple, sending sparks of awareness dancing through her. She flicked back and forth until it hardened.

She slid open the patio door and stepped inside, shivering a little as she stepped from the eighty-degree weather outside to the cool air-conditioned house. Both nipples tightened to hard nubs, but when she reached Matt's office door, she toyed with them to ensure both were hard and thrusting straight out. Then she knocked.

"Come in," he said.

She turned the doorknob and stepped into the room.

Matt sat at his desk, staring at the computer. He didn't even glance up when she entered.

"Hi," she said, leaning against the doorjamb.

"Hi," he said without looking up, totally engrossed in whatever was on his screen, his fingers flickering across the keyboard with a tapping sound.

She pursed her lips, but strolled across the room undaunted, her hips swaying. Not that he noticed.

"*I thought you might want a little break.*" *She stood beside him now.*

"*Not really. I'd like to work for another hour, then I'll be yours for the rest of the weekend.*"

She had no idea if he really meant an hour or if one would turn to four. He'd never brought work to do when he was with her before.

"*But I'd like you to be mine right now.*" *She crouched beside him and stroked her hand up his thigh.*

His eyes widened when he realized she was naked. But to her shock, he returned to typing on his keyboard. "*I'm afraid I have to keep working.*"

But the slight smile turning up Matt's lips tipped Kate off that he was toying with her. Not to be put off, she glided her hand over his crotch. The feel of the growing bulge under the fabric encouraged her. She stroked several times, then glided her fingers firmly along the sides of his shaft. The already-large bulge grew even more. It was rock-hard under her fingertips.

She grabbed the tab of his zipper and pulled it down slowly. The soft denim opened as she pressed her hand inside, then slipped it under the thin cotton boxers beneath until she found his hot, hard staff. Like molten marble.

She drew it out and gazed at it. Long and hard. Thin veins pulsing on the sides. She stroked it, from base to tip, then back again. She glanced at his face. His lips were tightly compressed as he continued to concentrate on the screen.

She shifted in front of him, shimmying under the desk since he continued to type. She leaned forward and pressed his big cockhead to her lips, then licked him. She thought she heard a groan, but when she glanced up, he was still staring intently at the computer screen. Her lips wrapped around his huge tip until it filled her mouth. She sucked and this time she definitely heard him groan. As she watched, he determinedly continued to type, but his fingers faltered as she glided down his hard shaft, taking him deeper. She squeezed as she glided away again, then sucked and licked the crown.

She loved having his cockhead filling her mouth. Loved squeezing it inside her. The tip of her tongue glided over it, then toyed with the small hole, tasting a salty drop of pre-come. It was definite evidence that he was interested. Not that the huge cock in her mouth wasn't a dead giveaway.

She drew it from her lips and stroked, his shaft warm and damp from her saliva. "I think you're ready for a break." Her lips curled up in a smile.

He gazed at her, but shook his head. "No, I really have to keep working."

If it weren't for the twinkle in his eyes, she would have been uncertain, but he was definitely toying with her. She drew her shoulders back in determination, then swallowed his cock into her mouth and began sucking in earnest. He swelled even bigger. She dove down as deep as she could, taking him down her throat, then she drew back. Down again, then back. Her fingertips found his balls and she stroked, then glided underneath and cupped them in her hand, all the while sliding his hard cock in and out of her mouth.

His balls tightened and she knew he was getting close. She could just continue and suck down the fountain that was sure to blow at any second, but she didn't. Not with him still typing away, though quite erratically now.

She grabbed the armrests of his chair and rolled it backward as she pushed herself out from under the desk. Then, holding his cock firmly in her hand, she turned her back to him and lowered herself until he pressed against her slick slit. Then she lowered herself the rest of the way onto his lap.

Oh, God, that marble-hard shaft felt like heaven gliding into her. It stretched her like no other had before. It was so long and so freaking thick. She groaned when she finally rested on his muscular thighs, then tightened her passage around him.

His typing had stopped, but then he had the nerve to start again. She glanced at the screen in front of him and smiled as she noticed everything he'd typed over the past few minutes was all gobbledygook. She took one of his hands and placed it on her naked breast, then pressed it hard against her. Her rigid nipple pressed deep into his palm. She took his other hand and pressed it to her mound, encouraging his finger to find her clit. His fingers moved frustratingly away and gripped her hips.

"You've displeased me by interrupting my concentration. Now I need to punish you."

She frowned. Really? For taking control this time? But the thought sent quivers through her. How would he punish her?

He grasped her waist and lifted her from his lap. His hard cock dragged along her sensitive passage, nearly sending her over the edge. Then it dropped from her and bounced upward as he set her on her feet. He stood up and grasped her shoulders, then guided her around the other side of his big desk. He swiped his arm across the surface, knocking everything to the floor. Papers, pens, desk accessories. Even his empty coffee mug.

Then he leaned her over the desk until her naked nipples pressed against the cold oak surface. A flattened hand on her back pressed her down harder, her breasts crushed against the hard wood.

"You are a very bad girl, disobeying my wishes like that."

He pressed his knees between her thighs and pushed her legs wider apart. His hand stroked over her behind, then slid between her legs. He stroked her wet slit several times, then she felt something hard and hot press against her. His cock pushed forward, and slid inside her.

"Do you like that?"

Oh, God, of course she did, but she wasn't sure if she should say yes or no. After all, this was to be a punishment.

When she didn't answer, he coiled his hand in her long, auburn hair and drew her head back until her neck curved against his shoulder.

"I asked if you like it?"

"Yes," she responded.

"Good, you're being truthful with me. I'll go easier on you this time." Then his cock slid away and he withdrew.

"No . . . please, Sir." Oh, God, but she needed him inside her.

"What was that?"

"Nothing, I'm sorry, Sir."

She heard his steps retreating. Oh, damn, he really was going to punish her by leaving her turned on and frustrated. She
drew in deep breaths, not daring to move. Hoping he would
come back.

Then he returned and she felt blazing hot, rock-hard flesh
press against her slick opening and drive deep inside her. She
cried out at the exquisite feel of his invasion. He pushed her
hard against the desk, his shaft pinning her from inside. Then
she felt his hand glide over her round ass, then between her
cheeks. He dipped a finger in beside his cock, then drew his
glazed digit upward until he found her other opening. He
pressed against it, then slid inside.

She sucked in a breath as he swirled his finger inside her
tight opening, his huge cock still filling her vagina. A spiral of
pleasure swept within her at each whirl of his finger. Rich, vi-
brant pleasure.

"Oh, God, that feels so good." She practically clamped her
hand over her mouth. Would he now withdraw again, to punish her properly?

But his cock was so hard, he must be aching to release
inside her.

He drew back, sliding his cock along her passage, sending a
quiver of intense pleasure through her. Then he drove impossibly

deep, his engorged cock filling her so full she thought she'd burst from the intense pleasure.

His finger slid from her ass and he grasped her hips. He began to thrust deeply. In and out until she felt as if she would pass out.

"Tell me how much you want me to fuck you," he demanded.

"Oh, yes, I do, Sir." She gasped as he jolted deep. "I want you to fuck me."

"Oh, God, Kate, you are so fucking sexy."

She gasped again as pleasure swelled through her. "Oh, yes. You're going to make me come."

"Fuck, yeah." He drove into her faster. "Tell me." He groaned as his cock stroked her insides. "Tell me when."

As his cock entered her again and again like a big, solid piston, she cried out, her passage clenching tight around him.

"Now, Sir." She gasped as pleasure expanded through her like a shock wave. "You're making me come . . . now." She wailed the last word as blissful sensations exploded through her.

Kate lay in her bed staring at the ceiling, her breathing heavy. Damn, she definitely missed the sex. But even when she'd tried to take control—even thought she had succeeded—he'd still managed to dominate her.

The next couple of weeks were hectic, but Kate didn't mind. Keeping busy helped keep her mind off Matt.

What kept her busiest was trying to find an investor for her company.

She sat at her desk, staring at the big red circle on the calendar two weeks from today. The contractual deadline to buy out her partner was fast approaching and if she didn't find an investor before then, she'd have to sell the business.

Her chest constricted. She really didn't want to do that. She'd worked hard to build up her small consulting firm, and it meant the world to her. It gave her a sense of accomplishment. It made her feel successful.

She'd moved to Connecticut two years ago because she'd needed the work. Things had been going well at the firm she'd worked at, but suddenly she'd found herself laid off. While she'd always been able to find consulting contracts before, they had suddenly become very scarce. A friend had told her about a project in Connecticut and, as much as she didn't want to leave New York, she'd finally had to face the fact that she had no choice.

The project had been perfect for her and her clients were extremely happy. They'd asked her to manage another, bigger, project, and soon she found herself bringing in other consultants to work under her. One of her associates suggested that they partner up and form a company and take on staff of their own. That was the start of her now-successful business, and she didn't want to lose it.

She stood up and walked to the window, then stared out at the snowy landscape beyond. What was she going to do? She'd worked too hard to make this business a success to lose it now. She clenched her fists. She had to find a way.

The phone rang and she crossed to her desk and picked up the phone.

"Kate, there's a Mr. Elliott, president of Facts and Figures Inc., on the phone for you."

She wasn't familiar with the company. "Thanks, Ann. Put the call through."

Ann connected them.

"Hello, Mr. Elliott. This is Kate Hayward. May I help you?"

"Yes, I understand you are looking for an investor. We've heard great things about your work and I would like to set up a meeting to discuss the possibility of our doing business together."

Her heartbeat accelerated. Could it really happen this easily?

Elation coursed through her, but concern followed on its heels. What if they insisted on a controlling interest? Or if they made demands she didn't want to meet?

"Of course. When would you like to meet?"

"How about this Friday?" he asked.

Kate circled the date on her desktop calendar. "That works for me."

"Fine. I'll have my assistant send over the details."

As Kate got ready for bed on Thursday night, her stomach fluttered at the thought of stepping into that meeting tomorrow, sitting in front of a group of high-powered executives and answering questions that would affect the future of her company. The representatives from Facts and Figures Inc. were coming in from New York and the meeting was set up for six o'clock in the evening. They had arranged all the details of the meeting, which was a relief since, with her partner leaving, her regular workload had doubled.

The weather was turning nasty overnight and the light snow was supposed to turn to freezing rain tomorrow. She hoped that wouldn't prevent them from traveling from the city.

Kate woke up to the sound of ice pellets hitting her window. By the time she got ready and stepped outside, it wasn't too bad. It had been above freezing overnight and was dropping now, but the ice melted when it hit the ground. If the rain kept up, though, it would soon start freezing to the pavement.

As the day wore on, the rain started and stopped. By

late afternoon, Kate stared out her window at the trees glazed in ice.

Ann walked into her office. "Hey, Kate, I just e-mailed you the information for your meeting this evening. They never did send me a complete list of the attendees. I think they weren't quite sure who'd be able to make it, especially given the weather," she said as she nodded to the window, "so I attached a list of their executives along with a bio for each one so you'll be prepared, no matter who shows up."

"Have you confirmed the meeting's still on?" Kate asked.

"Yeah. The car will pick you up here at five o'clock. They say the location is only about thirty miles from here, but they're allowing extra time for the bad weather."

"Okay. Thanks, Ann."

Ann smiled and headed for the door, then stopped in the doorway. "If I forget to say it before I leave, good luck. We're all counting on you."

Kate climbed into the long black limousine and felt the soft leather seat enfold her. She rested her head against the headrest and closed her eyes briefly as the car pulled away from the curb with a smooth thrust of power. The chauffeur had arrived at her office and identified himself as a representative of Facts and Figures Inc. with a photo ID and all, then led her to the sleek vehicle.

She longed to just relax and nap, since she'd slept so fitfully last night, but she wouldn't. She didn't feel it looked very professional.

At this time of year, it was already dark outside, so she couldn't see much out the windows. The lights of the city soon slipped behind them as the miles drifted by. She grabbed her cell phone and opened the e-mail Ann had sent her and began reviewing the bios of the executives of Facts and Figures Inc., but she quickly tired of it. She'd already been over them several times this afternoon.

She leaned forward and stared at the reflection of the driver's face framed in the rearview mirror. "Excuse me."

He glanced up and their gazes met in the glass.

"Where are we going?"

"To Erin Gate Manor, ma'am." He smiled politely. "It's a lovely spot, right on the lake. It'll be about forty-five minutes before we get there."

Some companies held their meetings at resorts where their executives could unwind and reduce stress levels between meetings. It sounded like this was such a place. In January, with snow carpeting the world and the temperature well below freezing, it would probably be lovely. Too bad she wouldn't be able to see it in the light.

The driver turned on some quiet music and she watched the snow-clad trees, glowing in the light of the moon, zip past along with the miles. When they finally turned off the main road, they drove along a densely treed road, which eventually opened onto a wide, curved driveway. The driver stopped the car, then got out, opened her door, and helped her out. Her gaze drifted over the warmly lit country house before her, drawn to the spectacular stained-glass panels on either side of the huge oak door. Although large, the house didn't look like a lavish resort.

She followed the chauffeur along the stone path to the entrance. Inside, a huge stone fireplace stood majestically in the center of the large room they entered, a welcoming flame licking at the wood logs behind the glass screen.

She slipped off her coat and thanked the driver as he hung it on a coat rack by the door. After he made his way out, she found herself alone in the large, quiet room, uncertain what to do next. It was clear as soon as she'd walked into the foyer that this wasn't a hotel or restaurant. It seemed more like a private residence. Maybe it had been easier to pull together a meeting at one of the executive's homes. It was a big place and would allow them the privacy to talk about financial matters, but in a comfortable setting.

She set her purse beside the couch, then wandered over to the fireplace, staring into the mesmerizing flames, letting the heat swirl around her.

"So, I see you're settling in."

Shock vaulted through her at the sound of that deep masculine—and very familiar—voice. She spun around, and came face-to-face with the one man she would have given anything to avoid.

Matt Pearce.

The Capture

Kate drew in a deep breath.

Matt Pearce stood on the other side of the enormous room, but he was far too close. His carefully controlled power filled the space, crowding around her. Her heart fluttered like a wild thing and her pulse throbbed at her temple in a rapid pounding. She grabbed onto the stonework around the fireplace to steady herself.

"What are you doing here?" she croaked.

His sensuous lips twisted into a smile. "I'm your new partner."

New partner. Oh, God, he must be the investor. She clasped her hands together because they'd started to tremble.

"But you're not on the list of executives for Facts and Figures Inc."

He smiled. "That's because I'm the owner."

Damn. She drew in a deep breath. "There's been no agreement signed yet. That's why I'm here, to see if we'll be a good fit."

A smile crept across his face. "As I recall, we're a *very* good fit."

His words sent a tremor through her, along with memories of his hot, hard body pressed tightly against hers.

She felt the heat of a blush creep across her cheeks.

He strolled toward her. "Surely the meeting is just a formality."

She couldn't stay here any longer. Being alone with him like this sent panic skittering through her. She glanced toward the door, assessing her chances of escape. She could fling caution aside and lunge around the couch, then race across the room toward the door, but he could catch up with her in three quick strides.

She sucked in a breath. Damn, she was overreacting. The man wasn't going to chase her.

Or would he?

"You look like you're thinking of fleeing. Is the thought of being here with me so distasteful that you feel you have to run away from me again?" he asked, the words strung as tight as his expression.

Whether he referred to the incident at the mall last

month, or when she had left him two years ago, she didn't know, or care.

"I want to leave right now," she demanded.

His lips compressed. "That's not an option."

Her eyes narrowed. "Why?"

"Well . . ."—he held his free hand out expansively— "we're at least a mile from the main road. It's the middle of January and freezing outside."

"The driver—"

"Is gone."

She glared at him. "So you're forcing me to stay here?" A chill ran through her.

"I had hoped you would stay long enough so we can talk."

A shiver ran down her spine. Did he want to talk to her about why he'd betrayed her two years ago? Not that he would think of it as betrayal. It was part of his way of life. To control his woman so completely.

Or did he want to talk to her about why she'd left? Her leaving must have been a surprise to him. He must have assumed she'd accept his complete domination or he wouldn't have planned the events that night.

A shiver rippled through her at the thought that he intended to keep her here against her will. Would he force her into submission?

She had never realized his desire for domination ran

so deep, until that fateful night two years ago when his true—and frightening—nature had been revealed.

Panic welled in her. He was bigger and stronger than her. With no difficulty at all, he could physically constrain her. Chain her to a wall or tie her to a chair. Flog her.

A flash of remembered pain ripped through her, but she pushed it aside.

His eyes narrowed as he watched her face. He stepped toward the fireplace. "I'm not stopping you from leaving, Kate."

His calm, reasonable voice dragged her from her panic.

She blinked, momentarily confused. "I don't understand. You just said—"

"I said the driver left." He picked up a brass poker and shifted the logs on the flames. Sparks flared violently. "That means you can't leave immediately. I told him I'd call him later this evening when we need him to come back." He gazed at her again. "After we've talked."

She tipped up her chin in defiance. "And if I don't want to stay and talk?"

He replaced the poker on the hanging stand and turned toward her. "I could call him to come back for you now, if that's what you want."

"Can't you drive me back?"

"I had a driver, too, Kate. I used the travel time to work."

"That's fine. Then I'll call a taxi."

He gazed at her with disturbing intensity. "Are you really so afraid of just sitting down and talking to me? What do you think I'm going to do?"

That was the problem. She really didn't know.

She drew in a deep breath. But if he intended to overpower her, he could have done it by now, and he could certainly stop her from calling a cab if he wanted to.

She was overreacting. After all, she'd walked away from him two years ago. Sure, he was probably angry about that, but they were no longer in a relationship, so his deep need to totally subjugate his woman didn't really apply to her anymore.

Unless he just wanted to see her powerless and squirming, to make her pay for escaping his control.

He strolled toward her. "You came all the way out here. Won't you even consider my offer to invest in your company?"

She felt confused and vulnerable. Over the past few months, she had exhausted every other avenue she could think of to get the money to buy out her partner, and the deadline was the end of this month. When she'd gotten that call from Mr. Elliott, the president of Facts and Figures Inc., saying they wanted to invest in her company, she had been thrilled, but now . . . She couldn't even imagine being in a partnership with Matt Pearce.

Her fists clenched at her sides. Damn, this was an impossible situation.

And getting worse the closer he got to her. Because despite everything that had happened between them, her heart still fluttered whenever she was near him.

And he was only a few steps away, and getting closer.

"I could use a drink," she said to stop him from drawing any nearer.

His eyebrows arched. "All right."

She suppressed a sigh of relief as he moved away, heading toward the built-in bar. He returned a moment later with a tall-stemmed glass of red wine for her and what smelled like rye whiskey for himself.

She avoided touching him when she took the glass, knowing she couldn't withstand physical contact and retain her composure.

She sipped her wine, watching him over the glass. "Why do you want to invest in my company?"

Her fingers tightened around the glass. He had wanted to control her, but he had failed. Did he now seek to re-establish that control by taking hold of her company?

Damn, she was small time compared to the big corporation he owned. Would he build some clause in the contract that would allow him to take controlling interest? Would he find a way to steal her company from her? This could be his revenge for her denying him what he'd wanted from her.

He swirled the amber liquor around the glass, his gaze intent on the rippling motion. "If it helps, I have no intention of getting involved in the day-to-day operation of a small consulting firm. You'll still retain control."

He had to be kidding. She never retained control when Matt was involved.

Damn it, even if he didn't have controlling interest, all he had to do was threaten to pull out his money and she'd be stuck. And he would know everything about her business because he'd have access to all her files. He'd be her *partner* for heaven's sake.

He sipped his drink, his dark eyes watching her over the rim of his glass.

Her breath locked in her lungs. Oh, God, she felt so trapped.

He simply stared, his face an emotionless mask.

But would he really steal away her company? The Matt she'd thought she'd known would never have done a thing like that. That Matt had been a kind, decent, caring man. A man who had once loved her. But then she had learned what he really was.

A man as powerful as Matt Pearce will never let you just walk away. So I suggest you run. Far. And fast.

That's what his friend Ileana had told her after that night. She had opened Kate's eyes to what he was. Her stomach clenched at the memory.

Now Matt would have the ability to control her company, and thereby control her.

She walked to the couch and sank onto it. The fire still crackled and blazed cheerily, but the warmth no longer touched her. A chill had started around her heart and now crept outward to encompass her whole being.

"Why are you doing this?"

His lips compressed. "Why do you think I'm doing it?" He sounded more quizzical than demanding and that confused her.

She shook her head. "I don't know. After what happened . . ."

Damn, she didn't want to get into it. Didn't want to hear him tell her why he'd been willing to subject her to that kind of pain.

His eyes narrowed. "What exactly happened, Kate? Between us?"

She stared at him in raging disbelief, then slammed her glass down on the coffee table and shot to her feet. "How dare you ask me that? After what you put me through . . ." The raging emotions flooding through her locked the breath in her lungs and words failed her. She paced across the floor.

"After what I put *you* through?" He placed his glass

on the mantel and paced toward her. "We really do have some talking to do."

"No." She slashed her hand through the air. "I don't want to talk to you about this. I don't want to hear your explanations."

His hard gaze sharpened. He stepped forward, his presence like a storm cloud descending on her, a turmoil of mixed emotions swirling in his eyes. He raised a hand and stroked her cheek with one outstretched finger. She forced herself not to flinch.

"Kate, was it my fault that you left? Did I . . . go too far with you?" The words came out soft and . . . uncertain.

She felt her composure crack as old feelings flared inside her. Heat suffused her cheeks and a longing she'd buried in the depths of her soul stirred. *No, don't let me feel this. I don't want to feel this.*

Oh, God, she knew she still loved him—because, quite simply, she'd never stopped—but she couldn't give in to the destructive emotion.

She stepped out of reach and turned away. Striding around the armchair to the fireplace, drawn to the flames and the warmth she wished would penetrate the numbness gripping her, she concentrated on collecting her composure.

She felt the fine hairs on the back of her neck stand up and realized Matt stood behind her.

"Kate, please tell me why you left."

She turned and stared at him in amazement. How could he ask her that? What he had done had been un-forgivable.

Her throat closed up and she couldn't have uttered a word if she'd tried. She wrapped her arms around her body, rubbing her hands up and down, trying to banish the dreadful cold.

"Damn it all, I loved you." He stepped toward her and she stopped herself from backing away. His hands clenched into fists at his sides. "Don't you understand? At first, I thought something terrible had happened to you."

The look of raw pain slashing his features shocked her. With all that had happened, she hadn't really thought her leaving would hurt him so much as it would make him angry.

And it seemed she had hurt him badly.

Now, seeing his vulnerability, her heart constricted. She longed to reach out and touch him. To stroke back the loose waves of hair that had fallen onto his forehead. To soothe away the pain.

His eyes narrowed. "Kate?"

Her name, soft and questioning on his lips, sounded too right. She wanted to hear him say it again, mur-mured in the dark shadows of the night. Her heart ached and hot moisture formed in the corners of her eyes.

"Kate?" he repeated. Concern etched his features.

In the softening of his eyes, she saw the Matt she had once known. The Matt she had loved. But she couldn't allow herself to fall for him again. Not knowing what he really was.

Yet she stood there, helpless, as he tipped up her chin and gazed at her with questioning eyes. She couldn't help but remember those blue eyes filled with desire. Her lips trembled.

He drew her face toward him, and captured her lips. Passion flared as his tongue glided between her lips, seeking the warmth inside. Clinging to her wits, she kept her teeth firmly clenched and slid her hands to his chest to push him away, but the warmth of the silk fabric under her fingertips, pulled taut across the hard muscles of his chest, sent her into a sensual whirlwind.

She opened to him, welcoming his tongue with her own. Her breasts swelled in reaction and she couldn't stop her tiny gasp of pleasure at being in his arms again. It took every scrap of will she possessed not to wrap her arms around him and melt into his embrace like hot honey. She wanted him so badly; needed him with an agony that transcended time and space.

Abruptly, he broke their embrace, holding her at arm's length, looking as shaken as she felt.

"Oh, God, Kate. Why did you leave me?"

The agony in his voice was too much to bear. Kate sucked in a gulp of air and jerked away from him, trying to pull herself together. Grabbing her wine, she took a swallow and concentrated on the cool, tart liquid washing down her throat. He snatched it from her hand and flung it across the room. Droplets flew from the glass like blood-red tears as it shattered against the ceramic-tiled hearth.

He grabbed her arms and pulled her toward him. The brush of his body against hers sent a shimmer of heated torment through her.

"I want an answer."

She could feel tension emanating from him in waves.

"Can't you see? I need to know." His words—tight beads strung out on a thread of anguish—shook her.

The depth of his emotion showed clearly in the way his hands tightened on her shoulders.

"Matt, you're hurting me."

Instantly, he loosened his hold, but he did not release her. His features sharpened into harsh relief.

This wasn't like Matt. The Matt she'd known had always been in total control of his emotions. Memories of time they'd spent together fluttered through her mind like a film stuttering through an old movie projector, hazy and erratic.

Of the way his lips would claim hers with potent authority. Of the way his touch could send her to ecstatic heights. And as they lay in bed together, their naked bodies entwined, of loving words murmured in his sexy, rumbling, bedroom voice. She wanted to throw herself into the strength of his arms and give herself to him.

It would be so easy to forget everything that had happened. To allow these feelings to sweep her away, and seek the comfort of his arms. To allow their passion to flare again.

He must have seen the surrender in her eyes. A shiver raced through her as his face moved toward hers.

A cell phone warbled.

She jerked back. What the hell was she doing?

His jaw clenched and he tugged the phone from his pocket.

"What is it?"

As he listened, she paced to the window, escaping the delicious heat of him.

"You're sure?" His gaze shifted to her. "Okay, tomorrow then."

He hung up the phone and shoved it back into his pocket. "That was our driver. The freezing rain has gotten worse and the weight of the ice on the trees has caused a lot of branches to fall. Apparently, the road out of here is blocked."

Oh, God, don't say what I think you're going to say.

"It looks like we're stuck here overnight."

Matt didn't understand why Kate was behaving so strangely. She stared at him as if he'd done something horrible to her, but she was the one who had walked away from their relationship. And without a word of explanation.

The last time he'd seen her, she'd been dancing with a man—another Dom—at Ileana's party. Later, Illy had told him Kate had left with the man. He'd been totally shocked. He never would have believed that Kate would behave that way. He figured Illy'd had it wrong, that Kate had just taken a cab home for some reason. Not that he understood why she'd do that, but it made more sense than her taking off with another man.

He had loved her, and he'd been sure she'd returned that love.

After the party, he'd called her. Days had gone by and she'd refused to answer any of his calls. He'd shown up at her apartment, but she wouldn't let him in. Not long after that, she'd moved away.

He'd always wondered if he should have dialed things back a bit with her. Although she had clearly loved being dominated, the Dom-sub relationship they'd fallen into had become intense and he could tell it had unnerved her a little. He was more experienced than she was, and he'd felt guilty that maybe he should have pulled back a bit.

But memories of her in his arms, begging him to give her pleasure, had overwhelmed him every time.

She'd thrown herself into the submissive role so completely.

Could that be why she'd had to get away from him? Did she blame him for going too far? Had she—reasonably so—expected that he, as the experienced one, would know how to balance things? Had he really been the one to cause their breakup? Sure, she'd been the one who'd walked away—and she shouldn't have done it the way she had—but maybe it was the only way she could find the strength to leave him.

Or maybe she'd simply been attracted to another, more intense Dom.

His heart ached at the thought of her in another man's arms. Of her begging *him* to pleasure her.

God, he had loved her so deeply. As he gazed at her now, he knew he still loved her.

The realization wasn't really a shock. After all, why else would he be here, willing to invest a huge chunk of money in his ex-girlfriend's business? A woman who'd torn out his heart and tossed it aside.

But no matter what had happened between them, he wanted to help her.

Given their past, he knew she might be reluctant to accept him as her partner, but she needed the money, and her company was a good investment. He had hoped they could find a way to get past what had happened between them and move forward. Maybe they still could if he could just get her to open up about why she'd left.

Kate's heart thundered in her chest. She did not want to stay here alone with Matt.

"Oh, no. I am *not* staying here overnight."

"We don't really have a choice. The driver can't get to us."

She glared at him. "Then I'll walk."

He just grinned. "You always were stubborn, but you know that's a bad idea."

She stormed to the front door and grabbed her coat from the coat rack, then pulled it on. "It's just below freezing. With a good coat, that's not too cold. And visibility's not bad." She fastened her buttons. "It's not like walking through a blizzard." She wouldn't get lost and die of exposure.

"And where exactly do you plan to go?"

"I'll walk back to the main road. A mile isn't that far. Then I should be able to get a cab. Or you can get your driver to meet me there."

"Are you really going to try walking out of here on the icy road? And in those boots?"

She glanced down at her high spike heels. She did wish she had her other boots. They were more practical, but she'd come here for a business meeting and she'd wanted to look her best, so these dressy boots were the right choice.

"I'll manage." She pulled on her leather gloves and threw him a defiant glare, then crossed the strap of her bag over her shoulder. "Are you coming?"

She really should just storm out of here on her own, but she was a bit leery about traveling out into the dark icy night on her own.

He shrugged, still with that annoying grin on his face, and walked to the closet by the front door where he retrieved his coat and pulled it on. He slipped on his gloves, then opened the front door for her.

The rain continued to fall, freezing on every surface it hit, glazing the already slick ice with a supersmooth finish.

As soon as her foot hit the porch pavement, it slipped forward. She steadied herself, then started to walk carefully, lifting each foot up, then placing it down again carefully as she walked. It had gotten *much* worse since the driver had dropped her off.

There were a few steps down to the path that led to the driveway. She grasped the icy railing and stepped down. As she shifted her weight, her foot slipped out from under her. Following closely behind her, Matt grabbed her arms and prevented her from crashing to the ground. He steadied her and set her back on her feet, then continued to grasp her arm. She wanted to pull away from him, but his hold on her gave her a sense of security. And she realized that with the icy path ahead, she was much more likely to get out of here with his help than without it.

She tried the next step and again slid forward, but with Matt's help remained on her feet.

They finally made it to the bottom of the three steps.

The whole path, steps included, were interlocking bricks. There was a shiny layer of sheer ice coating them. She tried to walk steadily along the path, but her feet kept wanting to slide out from under her.

"Maybe we should walk along beside the path," she suggested.

"Whatever you say." Still holding her arm, Matt guided her to the side of the path.

She lifted her leg and tried to jab her heel into the snow, hoping to get traction, but instead of punching through, her heel just scooted along the surface, and the force of the unexpected motion sent her off balance. She fell back against Matt, knocking him to the ground, with her on top of him.

Her body lay sprawled across his and she scrambled to stand up, but she couldn't get purchase. Her feet just kept sliding across the surface of the ice.

"Relax, Kate. Give me a minute."

He set her on his outstretched leg, so she was sitting on his thigh, then he slid off his coat and laid it on the ground beside her. He set her on the coat, then rolled onto his knees. She watched as he slid along the path to a cedar bush and grabbed it, then successfully pulled himself to his feet.

She could see the wet splotches growing on his shirt as the rain continued to fall. He'd given her his coat so she wouldn't get wet as she sat on the ground, but now he was out in the freezing weather without protection from the cold.

While continuing to hold on to the bush, he leaned down and grabbed the edge of his coat and slid her toward him.

"Kate, roll onto your knees, then I can help you up."

She did as he said. His coat protected her stocking-clad legs from the damp ice below.

He grabbed her arm and held on tight while she put one foot, then the other onto his coat, then pushed herself to her feet.

Once standing, she gazed down at his damp coat.

"Here, hang on to the bush," he instructed.

She grasped a handful of the evergreen branch and took a step off the coat. When she found a firm footing, she took her other foot off the coat. Then Matt picked it up. It was drenched.

"Kate, I'd offer to carry you, but we'd most likely wind up flat on the ground again. Why don't you just come back to the house?"

She glanced along the road that disappeared into the woods. A mile of this. Every step would be a challenge. It would take her forever to get back to the road, if she even made it at all. She might wind up sprawled in the ditch. She could hit her head, maybe get knocked unconscious. She could break her ankle.

No, it was too dangerous.

"Okay," she agreed reluctantly.

He tugged on his damp coat, then grasped her arm and she gingerly walked alongside him until they made it to the steps, then she clung to the railing as she proceeded up the stairs again, Matt right behind her. When they finally made it to the front door, she sighed in relief.

Matt helped her off with her coat and hung it on the coat rack, then hung his wet coat inside-out on another of the hooks. As she took off her boots, he crossed to the fireplace. He began releasing the buttons of his shirt and she stood mesmerized as the shirt opened up, revealing his sculpted chest and perfect abs.

"Uh . . . what are you doing?" she asked.

He glanced her way. "My shirt's wet. I'm going to hang it by the fire and warm up." He slipped the shirt from his shoulders.

"Oh." That's all she could manage, because he now

stood before her, naked from the waist up, in all his muscular glory. She found it difficult to breathe as she watched his muscles ripple as he grabbed another log and placed it on the fire.

"Do you want another drink to warm you up," he asked, "or would you like to just sit by the fire?"

Thoughts of sitting on the couch beside Matt—half naked and supremely masculine—in front of the fire sent heat of a different kind thrumming through her. It was so tempting to stroll over there right now, sit beside him, then nestle against his warm body. Let his arm curl around her. Snuggle in close. Let things progress naturally, which given her intense attraction to him, despite everything that had happened in the past, would lead to . . . bed.

Actually, they probably wouldn't make it to a bed. If she let things go the way her tingling body wanted, she'd be begging him to make love to her right in front of the fire.

"It's been a long day and I'm tired. I'd like to go to bed," Kate said.

"Are you sure? I didn't know if you'd have time for dinner before our meeting, so I have some food prepared."

"I ate something before I came." It was technically true, but all she'd had time for was a handful of celery sticks. Her stomach was rumbling, but she'd rather go to bed hungry than stay here with Matt.

"Okay." He smiled and walked toward her. "Well, then, let's get you to bed."

He picked up her purse and pressed a hand to the small of her back. She swallowed hard, wondering exactly what he intended as the pressure of his hand propelled her toward the magnificent spiral staircase. Did he expect to climb into bed with her?

Her anxiety heightened with each step as they ascended the stairs. Once they reached the upper floor, he led her down the wide hallway to the second door on the right and pushed it open. She hesitated, seeing the large canopied bed in lavender and white dominating the room. He ushered her forward and followed her in, placing her purse on the dresser.

She stood just inside the door, frozen to the spot, watching him. Did he intend to stay? Would he turn on his shockingly effective charisma in an attempt to convince her?

If he did, she'd be in big trouble.

He turned around and smiled, seemingly aware of her unease. Crossing his arms, he leaned back against the wall. "What is it, Kate? Nervous sleeping alone in a strange house? Don't worry. I'll be close by."

That's what she was afraid of. She moistened her lips with the tip of her tongue. "How close?" Her gaze fastened on the large queen-size bed.

He chuckled and stepped toward her. "How close would you like me to be?"

She ducked sideways and walked across the room. "How about China?" she grated.

He laughed again as he walked to the door. "Sorry. You'll have to settle for the room next door."

She heard the door click behind him. She waited a couple of heartbeats before she marched over and turned the key in the old-fashioned lock. Pulling it out, then clutching it tightly in her hand, she savored the feel of security, however temporary—the first she'd felt since Matt Pearce had walked into her life again.

She listened at the door and heard footsteps descending the stairs. She glanced around the sumptuous bedroom. The decor, dreamily feminine, appealed to her. Had Matt known it would? Had he cared?

Besides the double closet door and the door to the hallway, she noticed another door. Pushing it open, she found an en suite bathroom. Wonderful. She'd been worrying about leaving the security of this room to attend to her nighttime rituals.

She took off her suit jacket and hung it on the back of the desk chair. She'd love to take off her skirt, too—it was a bit damp from falling on the ice—but she didn't want to run around the room in just her pantyhose.

It was only eight o'clock. Although she'd told Matt

she was tired, that was only to escape his company. She doubted she would fall asleep this early. She walked to the big armoire across from the bed and opened it. Perfect. There was a TV inside.

She took the remote control and sat down in the upholstered armchair beside the bed. She'd love to change into something less stifling than this straight skirt and blouse, but . . . damn, she didn't have anything to change into. What would she sleep in?

The thought of sleeping naked with Matt in the next room made her uncomfortable. Which was silly. He was in the next room. He wouldn't come barging in here in the middle of the night.

Damn, she was falling into old patterns. She'd trusted Matt long ago . . . until that dreadful night. After that, how did she really know what he would do?

She heard footsteps walking down the hall again and she stiffened. She held her breath when they stopped outside her door. Was he going to barge in here right now? Would he decide to overwhelm her with his masculine presence, use his impressive authoritative aura to compel her back into her submissive role, then punish her for having left him?

A knock sounded on the door.

She stood up, staring at it. "What is it?"

"I thought you might like something to wear to bed," Matt said from the other side of the door.

"Um . . . no, I'm fine."

"I also have fresh towels for you, and a toothbrush and toothpaste."

She hesitated, not wanting to open the door, but she realized if he wanted to come in here, she couldn't stop him. The fact that he was asking her permission was a good sign, and she should respect that.

Also, she really wanted a toothbrush.

She crossed the room and unlocked the door. What would he have for her to wear, she wondered in trepidation? Some little frilly number? Or something in leather?

She pulled open the door. He stepped forward and she automatically backed up. But he simply passed her and set a tube of toothpaste and a toothbrush—still in plastic wrap—on the dresser, and set some fluffy white towels beside them. Then he laid something flannel on the bed.

"The pajamas will be too big, but you can wear the top as a nightshirt." He smiled. "Just like you used to."

Oh, God, she remembered wearing his pajama top as a shirt the first time she'd stayed over at his house. It had barely covered the essentials, but she hadn't worried about that. Not back then. Now, however . . .

"And here's a robe." Alongside the red flannel pajamas, he laid a burgundy velour robe. "You'll be swimming in that, too, but there's a belt, so it won't be too bad."

Her eyes narrowed. "Why do you have all these things if you didn't know we'd be staying overnight?"

"So suspicious, Kate. I didn't know *you'd* be staying overnight. I don't live nearby, remember. This is a place we use for our executives to stay when attending meetings at the financial headquarters. With the weather, I planned to stay over for the weekend. I have an extra pair of pajamas, and I'm letting you use my robe."

"Oh." She stroked the soft fabric of the robe. "Thank you."

"You're welcome. So if you haven't changed your mind about dinner, or a drink by the fire . . ." He raised a querying eyebrow.

Kate shook her head.

"All right. I'll leave you to it, then." He crossed the room to the door and opened it, then glanced back. "Good night, Kate."

"Good night," she murmured.

Then he closed the door behind him, leaving her alone in the room.

She breathed a sigh of relief.

She still couldn't believe Matt Pearce was back in her life. The reality of it shot through her brain like a bullet. What was she going to do? The only thing she could do was remain calm and wait him out—to see what he intended.

Why had he brought her here? Was he after revenge for his sullied male pride? But that wasn't the vibe she was getting from him.

She remembered the dark desire in his eyes after he'd kissed her this evening. A disquieting thought gripped her. Clearly, he'd brought her here to confront her about leaving him, but could he be hoping to convince her to start up their relationship again?

Taking a calming breath, she realized it was only her frazzled nerves and exhaustion talking. She put on the pajama top, did a quick wash-up, and slipped into bed. There was no reason for this fear rumbling in the pit of her stomach. Realistically, why would Matt want to pursue her? With his looks and wealth, he could have any woman he wanted. Why go after a woman who had rejected him so completely?

She yawned and realized she was more tired than she'd thought. Matt's pajama top was warm and cozy, and the subtle masculine scent of him surrounded her.

He was in the room right next to hers. Getting ready for bed. She remembered him stripping off his shirt downstairs, revealing his magnificent chest. Now he'd be removing his suit pants, stepping out of them, then walking to his bed in just his boxers. Or maybe he'd strip off the boxers, too, and climb into bed totally naked. Memories of his strong, virile body flitted through her mind. Desire trilled through her at the thought of his big cock swinging back and forth as he strolled to the bed. Who was she kidding? His cock was gigantic. An ache started as she longed to feel it inside her again.

It was dark and there was something cold and hard against her back, like a stone wall.

"Matt?" Kate called into the darkness, disoriented.

She blinked and it seemed to get lighter. She was in a room, like a dungeon. Cold stone walls surrounded her.

Panic rose in her. "Matt?" she cried.

She tried to step forward, but couldn't. She felt the bite of cold metal around her wrists. She glanced up to see solid metal bands around her wrist with chains attached to the wall. The chains clanked as she pulled at the restraints.

Matt, tall and wickedly handsome, walked toward her, wearing tight, black leather pants, his chest bare.

"Matt?"

His big shoulders bulged with muscles and the broad expanse of his chest was solid and smooth. Her gaze glided down to his tight, ridged abs. So sexy. Then further, to the bulge threatening to burst the seams of his leather pants.

She licked her lips.

He chuckled and leaned close to her ear. So close that when he spoke, his breath whispered across her neck, setting the fine hairs on her skin prickling to attention. "Like what you see?"

She wouldn't answer. She knew she shouldn't be with Matt. Knew she shouldn't want him.

But she did.

She wanted him to strip her bare and drive into her. Fill her deeply with his big, powerful shaft. Dominate her with his power. With his body. With the intense pleasure only he could give her.

He stroked her hair back, a gentle brush of his fingertips, and her skin rippled with awareness. His lips brushed lightly against her temple, his breath caressing her ear.

"Tell me you want me."

She shook her head. "No. I don't want to be with you."

He chuckled again. "Liar."

He eased back and his mesmerizing, deep blue eyes locked with hers. She couldn't look away, and she knew she couldn't lie, because she was sure he could see into her soul.

She tugged at the restraints again, needing to get away from him. "Let me go," she pleaded.

He leaned in close. "I'll never let you go," he murmured.

His words rippled through her, stirring a need deep inside. She knew there was some reason she should be afraid of him, that she should want to be free of these chains so she could get away, but this feeling, right now, of being totally under his control, sent her senses reeling. She wanted him to control her. She wanted him to *own* her.

He grabbed the collar of her blouse and tore downward. Her clothing seemed to disintegrate, then she was standing before him, totally naked. His big, masculine hands glided down her sides, then he nuzzled the base of her neck. Pleasure rippled through her.

"I should punish you for leaving me," he said, his lips brushing her collar bone with feathery light caresses.

"Is that why you brought me here? To punish me?"

He locked gazes with her again. "Yes." He moved away and picked up a flogger. Big, with multiple strips of leather.

Suddenly, she was facing the hard, stone wall, her wrists still chained. He wielded the flogger and it slashed across her back. But unlike the vaguely remembered pain of the last time she'd been whipped, the violent sensation erupting from the leather straps was mind-shattering pleasure. He whipped her again and she gasped at the intensity of it. He whipped her again and again. Her insides tightened and her body melted with desire. She could feel it dripping from her.

She gasped at the next strike. Waves of blissful joy washed through her.

He paused before the next strike and she sucked in a desperate breath, needing it so badly she wanted to cry out.

"Do you want more?" he demanded.

"Oh, yes, Sir. Please. More."

She gasped as the leather slashed her skin again, her body arching. Pleasure washed through her, rippling through every cell in her body. He kept on until she wailed her release, riding a wave of bliss that thrust her into pure ecstasy.

She fell against the stone wall, cold and hard. His hand brushed her shoulder and she found herself facing him again, her back against the cold wall.

He stroked her cheek with his finger. "Have you learned your lesson?"

"Yes, Sir." The words came out in a throaty murmur.

"And what have you learned?"

She gazed into his eyes, revealing her soul to him. "That I belong to you."

He smiled and she felt great satisfaction in the fact she'd pleased him.

Kate jolted from sleep. Oh, God, the dream had left her heated and filled with longing. She had to stop herself from leaping from the bed and racing to Matt's room. Banging on the door and begging him to take her. She could feel the moisture between her legs, desperately wanted him to glide into her with his big, masterful cock.

But she couldn't do that.

Oh, God, she was being a fool. She couldn't be with

Matt again. Couldn't give herself to him. The flogging in the dream had been pleasure itself, but she knew from experience that's not what it was really like.

What was wrong with her? How could she be so messed up?

For hours Kate lay in bed listening to the rat-a-tat-tat of ice pellets hitting the window and all she could think about was being in Matt's arms. She'd longed for him so much—had longed for him for the past two years. The dream about Matt had left her confused and full of turmoil. How could she want Matt so desperately after what he'd done two years ago? Emotions swirled through her as she lay in the dark room thinking about that dreadful night.

But it felt so far away now. Being near Matt again, the way he looked at her, the way she felt around him . . . God help her foolish heart, she found herself questioning if she'd been wrong about him. Maybe he wasn't guilty of the things Ileana had told her. Could Ileana have lied to her? Her gut clenched. But why would the woman have lied?

Her heart ached. Oh, God, she wanted so much to believe that Matt wasn't that warped person. That he really was the man she once believed cared about her above all else.

Who loved her as much as she loved him.

She longed to slip from this bed, go to his room, and climb into bed with him. To feel his strong, protective arms around her. And be loved by him again. To be made love to by him again.

Her fingers curled around the edge of the duvet and she clung to it tightly as butterflies flitted through her stomach.

But if she went to him, would he hurt her?

Her thoughts continued in circles as she tossed and turned, but finally the blanket of sleep surrounded her, like a thick, fuzzy wrap that insulated her from the world. As she snuggled into its warmth, her anxiety slipped away.

She felt herself floating. Drifting through nothingness. The silence, mingled with the dark, gripped her, engulfing her. It pressed against the pupils of her eyes, filling her ears, leaving her sightless and deaf because no light or sound could penetrate.

Only darkness. And silence.

The nothingness around her shifted, until she felt hard concrete beneath her bare feet. She opened her eyes. Darkness surrounded her. She blinked several times as, slowly, her eyes grew accustomed to the lack of light. She could barely make out her surroundings. A small, dim room. Stone walls and floor. She became aware of a biting pain around her wrists and an ache in her arms and shoulders. Her arms were suspended above her head and when she tried to pull them down, she couldn't. At a clinking noise above her, she glanced up. Chains, linked to metal bands encircling her wrists, disappeared into the darkness above her.

The memory of Matt walking out of the darkness, then pleasuring her until she cried out in ecstasy prickled through her brain, but this was different. A chill crept the length of her spine, rippling outward to her fingers and toes.

Someone laughed behind her. A familiar laugh she hadn't heard in a long time. Deep and frightening. Chilling her to the core.

She heard a snap, then a line along her back exploded in pain. Another snap and more pain.

"No," she cried.

The man behind her simply laughed again. The leather whip bit into her flesh a third time.

"Please. Stop." Tears ran from her eyes at the biting pain. Still he slashed the whip against her back. Her legs gave out and she hung from the chains. The metal bands bit into her wrists, tearing at her flesh.

He whipped her again and again. The agony lanced through her, finally leaving her numb.

Matt was responsible for this. He had heartlessly arranged this. Planned to do the same thing to her himself later. But for now, he wanted this man to inflict pain on her. To teach her to submit fully. To make her understand what punishment she would suffer if she did not submit completely.

The man turned her around and pushed her against the wall behind her, slamming her wounded back against the cold, hard stone. She cried out at the pain.

He stared at her with cold eyes and pressed his arm against her throat until she couldn't breathe. She struggled against him, trying desperately to suck in air, but she couldn't. Panic gripped her as she felt blackness surrounding her. Terror arched through her and a scream welled within her.

Kate bolted upward as the scream tore from her throat. Her head jerked around as she tried to comprehend where she was. Moonlight streamed across the room and she realized she was sitting up in bed.

"Kate, what the hell?" The door flung open and Matt stormed into the room.

His gaze locked on her and he raced toward her.

She skittered back until she was pressed tight to the headboard, her eyes wide. As Matt closed in on the bed, she shook her head in panic. "No."

Matt halted, staring at her with a narrowed gaze.

"Kate, what's wrong?"

"I . . ." Suddenly, all the pain and anguish from that horrible ordeal burst through her and tears flooded from her eyes. "How could you do that to me?"

He sat down on the bed and reached for her, but she shifted sideways, putting more distance between them. His hands rolled into balls. "Do what, Kate?" He gazed at her with kind, tender eyes. "It was just a nightmare."

"No." The word came out hoarse and shaky. "It wasn't. It really happened. *You* made it happen."

"What, Kate? What do you think I did?"

"That night . . . at the party . . . you . . ." She sucked in a breath of air, steadying herself. "You *sold* me to that man."

"What the hell are you talking about?"

Kate flinched at his sharp words.

"Kate," he said more softly, "I really don't know what you mean. Why do you think I sold you to someone?"

"Your friend . . . the hostess . . ."

"Ileana?"

She nodded. "She told me it was part of the role-playing that evening. That you had arranged for me to submit to a man named Victor."

"Was that the man you disappeared with that night?" he asked with gritted teeth.

She nodded again.

"What did he do?" Matt's voice was nearly a growl.

"He . . . took me to a room. Like a cell with stone

walls. It was in the basement of the big house where the party was."

"Did he hurt you?" Matt's dark blue eyes blazed with anger, but she knew it wasn't at her, and confusion swirled through her.

She nodded. Then she couldn't look at him anymore. Despite her swirling emotions, the indignation in his eyes made her insides churn. Oh, God, could she have been wrong about Matt's involvement? But both Ileana and Victor had confirmed that Matt had set up the whole thing. And Ileana was Matt's friend. Why would she lie?

"Kate, believe me, I would never have allowed such a thing if I had known. That night, Ileana spirited you away to show you the house, then other than seeing you dance briefly with that man, I didn't see you again. Ileana told me you left with him."

"No, he chained me up. He . . ." She shook her head, unwilling to think about it again. "Ileana arranged a ride for me afterward. She told me you'd left already."

His blue eyes turned icy. "That lying little . . ." He mumbled the final word, then turned to her. The cold blaze of anger in his eyes turned to warmth as he gazed at her. "Kate, believe me. Whatever happened to you that evening, it had nothing to do with me. I promise you that. And if I'd known about it, I would have killed the bastard." He practically growled the last words.

She sucked in a breath at the sincerity in his voice.

Could it be true? Had she been wrong all this time? Her heart ached at the possibility.

He reached out to her and she hesitated, then placed her hand in his. It was so big and strong. So comforting.

"Come here, Kate." He drew her forward and swept her into his arms. His embrace was heaven on earth.

She felt safe cocooned there, close to his solid body, his hand stroking her hair. Tears fell from her eyes and she found herself sobbing against his chest. Releasing all the pent-up pain that had been deep inside her for two years now.

"So that's why you left?" His voice was stiff and constrained. "You thought I was some kind of monster?"

The Revelation

Kate drew away and gazed up at Matt. The agony in his deep blue eyes sliced through her.

"I'm so sorry, Matt. I didn't mean to hurt you." She stroked her hand along his whisker-roughened cheek.

He nodded, but shifted back. His arms slipped away from her. She missed the warmth of them, the feeling of security they gave her.

"Are you okay now?" His voice sounded flat and his eyes showed no emotion.

"I . . . think so." But she wasn't. Confusing emotions swirled through her. For so long, she'd believed that Matt was responsible for the pain she'd suffered. That Matt was a ruthless, uncaring man. But now she knew the truth.

And she'd been horribly wrong. A sharp pain started in the pit of her stomach and spiraled through her.

The look of betrayal she'd seen flash across his eyes before they'd blanked of all emotion tore at her heart.

She had to get used to the idea that Matt had done nothing to drive her away. Yet she had left him, suddenly and with no explanation. He had thought she'd just walked away from their relationship.

Her hands curled into balls. Oh, God, he must have hated her.

"I think we should both get some sleep." Matt stood up and walked toward the door.

"Matt . . ."

He paused, but didn't turn around.

"I . . . I'm sorry."

He simply nodded and left the room.

As exhausted as Kate was, sleep did not come soon. Random thoughts swirled through her head in an erratic whirlwind, with no beginning and no end. She flipped back and forth restlessly while the mocking blue digits of the clock ticked off the minutes.

How could she have ever believed that about Matt? But at the time, she'd trusted Ileana. And why not? She'd been the hostess of the party. She'd been Matt's friend. The party had had a BDSM theme, with people dressed as Masters and slaves. It had seemed like a game at first, going with Victor. He'd seemed charming, yet authoritative. When she'd followed him from the dance floor, she'd thought they would do some harmless role-playing. She'd never dreamed he would lead her to a cell and chain her up. Even then, she'd remained relatively calm, still assuming it was role-playing . . . and assuming he would stop if she said so. But he hadn't even offered a safe word. As soon as she'd seen the leather whip, she'd told him she wanted to end it, but he'd just laughed. Then as he began to whip her, he'd ignored her cries of protest.

It had been a nightmare, and he had kept insisting it was Matt's idea—to teach her to be a proper submissive. With each slash of pain, he'd beat the idea into her. Matt wanted this. He'd arranged it. Ileana had reminded her of it afterward when Kate had been limp with pain and anxiety. Ileana had arranged a ride home for her, but before she'd let her go, she'd given Kate a friendly caution that maybe she should steer clear of Matt if she really didn't like this kind of thing, insinuating that she was surprised at Kate's negative reaction to being beaten.

Kate had decided then and there that the lifestyle Matt was into—reinforced by Victor's obvious pleasure at hurting her, and Ileana's apparent surprise at Kate's fear and anger over the event—was a horrific thing. It had also made her believe that Matt had to be a ruthless and cruel man who had totally fooled her. In her weak and confused state, her blurry mind couldn't help but believe that about him. She could find no trace of the trust she'd once had in him.

Tears pricked at her eyes at how wrong she'd been. Not only had Matt not betrayed her, she had betrayed *him*. One, by believing what she had about him. And, two, by walking away without a word. Without even telling him what happened.

She realized now that she'd probably been so quick to flee without confronting him because she'd been afraid of his effect on her right from the beginning. Of what she became around him. She became weak and vulnerable. She would have let him do anything to her.

Now, she felt sick at the realization that she had hurt him. Badly.

He was angry with her, and he had a right to be. She'd walked away without a word. But worse, she had believed such a terrible thing about him.

She wished she knew how to make it up to him.

Tomorrow, the driver would come and pick her up and she might never see Matt again. Oh, God, maybe he'd been serious about wanting to invest in her company. Until now, she'd thought it was just a ruse to get her here, but now that she knew he was not the ruthless man she'd thought he was, she realized that maybe his offer to invest was genuine. Which must mean he still harbored feelings for her.

And now that he knew what she'd believed about him, he wouldn't want to have anything to do with her or her company.

She sighed. She'd find another investor. She had to. She wouldn't expect him to work with her after this. But she didn't want to leave things the way they were between them.

She drew in a deep breath and pushed back the covers, then padded across the room. Her insides quivering, she opened the door and headed for Matt's room.

Moonlight from the almost full moon outside reflected off the snow, setting the room aglow in a soft light. Matt stared at the ceiling, aching inside, still reeling from Kate's revelation about what had happened two years ago.

Fuck, when he'd heard her screaming, he'd leaped from his bed and flown to her room. In her sleep-hazed terror, when she'd awoken and seen him, she'd been afraid of him, accusing him of having hurt her. His gut clenched at the fact she could ever think he would hurt her.

And then he'd found out she'd thought he'd sold her to another man, as part of a role-playing scenario. Sure, that kind of thing happened. Some people liked to push. A different hand to bow to, a different sub to control. Sometimes it was just for the discipline aspect, sometimes it was for full-out sexual intimacy. He raked his hand through his hair. But he never would have shared Kate with anyone. She was his.

She *had been* his, anyway.

He had loved her deeply. Completely. Yet she'd obviously never trusted him.

Matt heard a knock at the door. What the fuck?

He rolled onto his side. "Come in."

The door opened and there, silhouetted in the moonlight streaming in from the hallway window, stood Kate. She stepped forward and he could see the pajama shirt she wore hugging her body. Her breasts bounced softly as she walked across the room. The shirt hung to midthigh, leaving a good portion of her long, lithe legs visible. His heart thumped faster having her in his room like this. No bra. Possibly no panties. Only a soft shirt with buttons down the entire front. Not that he'd bother with those buttons if he were going to make love to her. He would rip that shirt off her so fast, her head would spin.

"What do you want, Kate?" He leaned over and turned on the lamp on the bedside table, then he pushed his legs over the side of the bed and sat up.

She gazed at him the whole time she walked toward him, her eyes big and full of emotion. Sadness? Pain? Fear? His heart clenched. Was she afraid of him?

Well, fuck, she thought he was the type of man who would hand her over to another man as a slave, without even telling her about it. Damn, no wonder she'd acted so strangely this evening. When she'd demanded to leave and he'd told her they couldn't go anywhere until the driver returned, she'd probably believed he had intended to trap her here. God, no wonder she had been so jumpy, her eyes filled with panic.

And that's why she'd run from him in the mall.

Good God, Kate actually believed—his heart ached— that he would hurt her.

His hands curled into fists. How could she ever believe that? He loved her and would do anything to protect her.

He wanted to grab her and shake some sense into her. To scream at her that he would never, ever hurt her.

He wanted to pull her into his arms and kiss her with all the passion and desire he had locked inside. To claim her mouth, totally and completely, to show her just how deeply he loved her.

She stood by the side of the bed now. "I . . ." Her hands hung by her sides and her fingers curled tightly. "I'm here because . . ."

Her hesitance tore at his heart.

"Damn it, Kate. What the fuck do you want?"

She flinched. Damn, he hadn't meant to speak so sharply, but she threw him off balance. He wanted her so goddamned much.

Fuck, she held all the power. He'd been a damn fool to bring her here. To subject himself to this kind of pain again.

He drew in a deep breath and tried again. "Just tell me what you want, Kate."

"I . . . I know it wasn't fair that I left two years ago . . . without telling you . . ."

She hesitated, clearly uncertain. A long silence fell between them.

Watching her now . . . seeing her vulnerability . . . his heart clenched. Ever since he'd strode from her room, he'd only thought about himself, and his pain. But now he thought about her gut-wrenching scream. He didn't know exactly what happened to her that night at Illy's, but clearly it had traumatized her.

Fuck, what had the guy done to her? He'd been so angry that Kate hadn't trusted him that he'd blanked out thinking about what Kate might have endured. Did the guy have sex with her? Did he overpower her? His heart thundered in his chest as his heart rate accelerated.

"Kate, what happened?"

Her questioning gaze flicked to his. "As I said, Ileana lied to me and told me—"

He held up his hand to stop her words. He didn't need to hear it again. "What did this man do to you?"

Her gaze immediately dropped from his and his chest compressed.

"I . . . really don't want to talk about it."

Fuck. She'd turned white as a sheet. An overwhelming protectiveness jolted through him.

"Well, *I* really need to talk about it." He patted the bed beside him. "Come and sit down."

She drew in a deep breath, but stepped forward and sank onto the bed beside him.

"He took me to the room I told you about. In the basement. It had a thick door and the walls were of big, concrete bricks. He chained me to the wall."

She spoke in a halting voice, clearly struggling with telling him, but she obviously felt she owed him this.

"Did he . . . force you to have sex?"

She shook her head. "Nothing like that. He made me face the wall before he chained me up. I thought he was just playacting at first. That it was a game. He said he was going to punish me."

Matt and Kate had often played the punishment scenario, and it made him jealous now that she had even agreed to play a scenario with someone else, but she'd already told him she'd thought he had arranged it, so essentially she'd done it to please him. And if Ileana had told her Matt had ordered her to do it, she would not have argued.

"And he did," Matt said.

Kate just nodded while she stared down at her hands.

"Tell me."

"He used a whip. It . . ." She hesitated, then swallowed. "I never realized how much a leather whip would hurt."

Damn it. She must have thought Matt a monster to arrange such a thing.

"God damn it, Kate, how could you believe I would even allow such a terrible thing to happen to you, let alone arrange it?"

She gazed up at him, her eyes shimmering. And, to his surprise, a little defiance flickered in those blue depths. "You did let it happen."

"What the hell are you talking about?"

"You're angry with me because I believed you'd let it happen, yet you believed Ileana when she told you I'd left with another man. If you hadn't believed her, then maybe you would have looked for me. Maybe you could have stopped it." The vulnerability in her eyes tore at his heart. "Matt, why did you think I would do that?"

Damn it. The woman had no right to turn this around on him. "The evidence was there. You clearly enjoyed dancing with the guy. You disappeared with him after that. And when I still gave you the benefit of the doubt and tried to talk to you afterward, to find out exactly what did happen, you wouldn't take my calls."

Her lips compressed in an appropriately contrite expression, and he realized he couldn't leave the blame hanging on her.

"And it didn't help that I already felt you were slipping away from me. I sensed you wanted to end it between us for some time, but something held you back. So when I saw you in that man's arms on the dance floor, then when Illy told me you had left with the guy . . . it seemed to confirm my worst fears."

Guilt prickled through him. He'd handled so many things badly with Kate. Let things get out of control. And it had led to disastrous results for her in so many ways.

Kate gazed at his enigmatic, dark eyes. He knew about that?

She drew in a deep breath. "I was a little thrown off by things."

He raised an eyebrow. "Things?"

She stared at her hands. "I mean . . . sexually. The way I"—she gazed at him and shrugged, realizing she just had to state it outright—"you know . . . become totally submissive to you. Giving up every scrap of control."

"Kate, you can't tell me you didn't like it."

"Obviously I liked it." There was no way she could deny that. "But I don't *want* to like it. I don't like what I become."

His lips compressed. "So you wanted to end the relationship before we even went to that party."

His tone didn't betray any hurt, but she knew him well enough to know she'd struck a nerve.

She drew in a deep breath while he watched her, waiting. But what could she say? It was true.

"Matt, it wasn't you, it was me."

"Fuck." His eyes glittered with anger—or was it pain?—then he stood up and walked across the room.

"Matt, I know that's a cliché, but in this case, it's true. You're comfortable with who you are, and that's good. You dominate in the bedroom, and clearly that turns me on immensely. But it also frightens me. The way I become. I . . ."

But talking to his broad back unnerved her. Was he even listening?

She stood up and walked to him, then rested her hand on his shoulder. "Matt, please look at me."

He sighed and turned around, his face an emotionless mask.

"I'm sorry I believed what I did about you. That I didn't take any of your calls. I shouldn't have taken her word for it, but . . . at the time, I was so . . . so . . ."

Suddenly, the whole thing came crashing back to her. The fear. The pain. And the devastating sense of abandonment and betrayal when Ileana had told her Matt had been responsible for what had happened. She sucked back a sob.

But the bottom line was, Matt had done nothing wrong, yet she had caused him immeasurable pain.

"I'm sorry I hurt you," she said in a mere whisper. She gazed into his midnight blue eyes, mesmerized by the intensity of his stare, and she had to touch him. She stroked his cheek with her hand.

At the feel of his whisker-roughened skin under her fingertips, at the warmth of his body so close to hers, heat washed through her.

"Matt, I'm sorry. I never should have allowed Ileana's lie to shatter my trust in you, but . . . what that man did . . ." Her words faltered as she remembered the harsh lines of the man's face as he'd chained her to the wall, then the sharp slash of the whip against her skin.

"Kate . . ."

She drew in a deep breath and pushed her shoulders back. "I don't understand why Ileana lied to me, or that stranger did what he did, but . . . I never should have believed them." She gazed at Matt, willing him to see into her soul. "I want you to know that I do trust you."

Anger blazed in Matt's eyes. "If I had known what was happening . . ." His hands clenched into fists. "If I had gotten my hands on the guy . . ."

He wasn't hearing what she wanted him to hear. She wanted him to understand—to believe—how deeply she did trust him. The man at the party had drawn on her trust of Matt, and betrayed it. Despite what happened to her, if Matt wanted to chain her to the wall now, she would totally trust him. She knew he would never hurt her, even if he wanted to punish her. Because his punishment always led to shared pleasure.

Her insides heated at the memory of Matt's hand slapping across her ass, leaving her skin tingling.

Maybe she could prove to him just how much she trusted him.

"Matt, never mind that now." She held out her hand. "Come with me."

He watched her for a moment, his glinting gaze piercing through her. Then he took her hand.

Oh, God, the feel of his strong, masculine fingers wrapped around her smaller ones sent heat pumping through her. His bedroom was huge, and she led him to a big couch facing the large window that overlooked a ravine behind the house. Moonlight cascaded over the icy landscape, illuminating it in a soft, white glow.

She walked to the back of the couch and released his hand, then she leaned over the couch, slowly drawing up her nightshirt as she bent over. She could feel the cool air on her naked behind. She only wore a thong, so he would have a full view of her naked ass.

"What the hell are you doing?" Matt had trouble keeping his voice steady with her leaning over the back of the couch, her deliciously round, naked ass totally exposed.

"Punish me, Matt."

His pulse quickened and his fingers itched to reach for her. To stroke along that smooth, white flesh.

Fuck. "But, Kate, after what you went through . . ."

"I trust you, Matt. I know you'd never hurt me."

Her words reached inside him and tore at his heart. How could he turn down her show of trust?

He stared at her creamy, round flesh, the moonlight caressing it in soft light. He stepped closer, unable to resist the need to touch her, his cock swelling painfully.

But he shouldn't get involved with her physically, since starting a romantic relationship with her again was not an option. Having sex, or whatever this would be, was a bad idea. A really bad idea.

But she trusted him. And this would be a healing step for her—to get past what that guy had done to her. He couldn't say no.

Fuck, he didn't want to say no.

As Kate felt him draw near, she thought she might feel anxiety, given her experience with Victor, but she really did trust Matt. Completely.

She felt Matt's hand on her ass. She expected an immediate slap, but instead, he stroked. Gently. Tenderly. His big hand cupped her, then glided sideways. As he stroked her buttocks, heat washed through her at his masculine touch. He was so big and strong. She wanted him to touch more of her. Her nipples peaked at the thought, and her insides tightened.

Then his hand drew away. Suddenly, it smacked across her ass, making her gasp. It didn't hurt, but it smarted. Her skin tingled where his hand still rested against her.

Then he drew back his hand and smacked her again.

Her gasp sent heat thrumming through him. His cock swelled even harder. He smacked again, then left his hand resting on her heated skin. Her ass was so round and perfect. He raised his hand and smacked again.

He could hear her accelerated breathing. She was turned on. He smacked again and she gasped again, then moaned.

"Do you like this, Kate?"

"Oh, yes, Sir."

Oh, fuck. His cock jerked to full mast. He wanted to drive into her so badly.

"Do you want me to keep spanking you?"

"Yes, please, Sir." She squirmed, her glowing red ass beckoning to him.

———

Kate couldn't believe how this made her feel. His smack stung, making her skin tingle. And she wanted more. Excitement churned through her and she could feel the moisture pooling between her legs.

"Please, Sir, punish me."

Matt stifled a groan. Her words were killing him, sucking the strength from him. She *owned* him. But he didn't care right now. He wanted to give her what she wanted.

He smacked her again and she moaned. Again and again his hand clashed with her flesh, the smacks sounding loudly in the silence of the room.

"Oh, yes." Her breathy words ground through him.

God, he wanted her right now. He would love to pull aside the crotch of her thong and drive right into her. But he wouldn't. That's not what she'd invited him to do. He smacked again and her ecstatic moan thrilled him.

He sensed she was close to orgasm. He didn't know if the spanking would take her all the way there or not. And he didn't want to keep hitting her. To bring her release, he'd have to go harder, faster. Her skin already sported an angry redness.

He wanted to caress her. To bring her pleasure. So as he smacked her again, he stroked her ass with his other hand. Then glided his fingers between her legs. Fuck, she was wet. He smacked again as his fingers slid beneath the crotch of her thong.

Kate's breath caught as she felt his fingers glide under her thong. He smacked and she cried out, then the rising pleasure blossomed as his fingers slid over her slick opening. She gasped at his sure stroke, pleasure pummeling through her. *Smack.*

"Oh, Sir. Oh—" She gasped as he found her clit. "Oh, please, yes." She sucked in air as his fingers glided inside her, his other hand smacking again. Her whole body vibrated in need as she relinquished herself to him. A swell of intense sensation rose within her and she moaned her release. Ecstatic joy blasted through her and she arched against his hand, then wailed. The agony of her release shattered through her.

Matt couldn't believe the intensity of her orgasm. He practically ejaculated on the spot. But he held it back. That wasn't what this was about.

But what was it about? Did she just want to assuage her guilt for walking out on him? Did she just want to get off?

Two years ago, he'd been sure she'd been as in love with him as he was with her, but he'd grown to realize that wasn't true. And she hadn't denied it a few minutes ago when he said he'd believed she'd wanted to end the relationship with him.

But right now, he felt close to her. Just like he had before. He felt *love* for her.

Damn fool that he was.

He put his hands on her waist and drew her to her feet. She turned and faced him. Her face was aglow. Soft. Feminine. Radiant from the pleasure he'd just given her.

God, he wanted her so badly.

She gazed deep into his eyes and seemed to recognize his need. She tipped her mouth up. The tip of her tongue glided over her lips.

Fuck, he couldn't help himself. He took her in his arms and kissed her. Her soft mouth yielded to his. He drove his tongue into her, needing to possess her.

Kate melted against him. He took her mouth with confidence, his tongue gliding deep, exploring her with authority. Her insides ached in need. Her nipples drove into his chest, longing for his attention.

But there was something she needed even more.

His mouth withdrew and he gazed down at her.

"Fuck, Kate, the way you're looking at me . . ."

"I want you to . . ." She drew in a shaky breath. "I need . . ."

His hands tightened around her shoulders.

"What is it? What do you need?"

She couldn't just ask him. But . . . she could . . . beg. Like she'd done so often in the past.

"Please, Sir. I want you to fuck me."

His eyes clouded and he hesitated, but he didn't draw away.

She stepped back and stripped off her thong, then leaned over the couch again, offering herself.

She heard him release a pent-up breath. He stepped behind her and she expected his hard cock to drive into her.

Instead, he took her shoulders and drew her upward, then turned her around so they were face-to-face and pulled her into another heart-shattering kiss.

His lips parted from hers and he gazed at her with a fierce expression. "Tell me again what you want."

He seemed close to losing control and that thrilled her. "Please, Sir, I want every inch of you inside me."

And she did. God, her insides ached with the need to feel him inside her. Stretching her. *Filling* her.

He dropped his pajama pants to the floor, then backed her against the wall so fast she gasped. His fingers found her opening and stroked.

"Oh, yes."

He groaned, then hard, hot flesh pushed against her. His cockhead teased her opening.

"Hard. Drive into me hard, Sir."

His fierce glare, shimmering with defiance, cut through her. Would he refuse?

But he drove into her, his hard column of flesh impaling her in one sure stroke.

He held her tight to his body, crushing her against his broad chest. "Is that what you want?"

"Yes, Sir," she said with a slow breath. Oh, God, she'd almost forgotten how long and thick he was. Almost. Her body remembered, and embraced him. She quivered as they stood there, his big cock deep inside her, his body crushing her to the wall.

He gazed down at her and the intensity of his dark blue eyes unnerved her.

Almost as if . . . No, she wouldn't believe that he loved her.

She squeezed him with intimate muscles and he groaned.

Matt couldn't help himself. She squeezed and he responded. He lifted her legs and she wrapped them around him, then he drew back and drove deep again. Deep into her hot velvet depths.

"Oh, yes."

Her words, dripping in pleasure, rocked through him. He didn't know how long he'd last. He was so close, so delirious with need being inside her like this.

Her fingers tightened around his shoulders as he drove in again and again. His cock ached as the cool air surrounded him, then he drove into her hot depths again. Cool, hot, cool, hot. She arched against him and moaned. He gritted his teeth, willing himself to hold back. Just long enough . . .

"Oh, God, yes." She threw her head back. "Oh, yes . . ." Her fingers tightened. "You're making me . . ."

Her passage tightened around him as she shuddered in orgasm. He thrust deep and let go. His balls tightened and heat coursed through him, flooding into her.

He held her soft body tight to him as he came. The intensity of it heightened every sensation. Her nipples pressed into him. Her hot sheath around him. Her soft breathing against his neck. The thumping of her heart against his chest.

He held her close, never wanting to let her go.

But knowing he had to.

He gazed down at her and her eyelids fluttered open, revealing her big, beautiful blue eyes. Their gazes locked, then her eyes widened and . . . Oh, fuck, he could sense her drawing away. The open, vulnerable look in her eyes closed and her body tensed ever so slightly.

But her heart still beat close to his, and her hot sheath still surrounded him.

He wasn't willing to give up this closeness again. Not yet.

He captured her mouth, swirling his tongue against hers, then he swept her into his arms and carried her to his bed.

Kate's breath caught as Matt laid her on his bed. She didn't know what to think. Didn't know what to feel. Having Matt inside her again, making love to her . . . Oh, God, it had been sheer heaven. But then when she'd opened her eyes and seen him staring down at her . . . What did he think? She didn't dare to believe he would want her again.

Sure, he'd made love to her, but any man would take an opportunity like that. A woman offering sex . . . why would he say no? But for her, it had been so much more. After two years of believing the worst of him, and now finding out it was all a lie, she realized Matt really was the man she'd fallen in love with back then.

He drew her against his body, spooning her, his arms wrapped around her waist. The staccato patter of ice pellets hitting the window signaled the return of the freezing rain, but she'd never felt so warm or so protected, curled up tight against Matt's big, hard body with his strong arms around her.

She sank into the heaven that she found herself in and soon fell sound asleep.

Matt held her close, loving the feel of her soft, warm body close to his. She hadn't intended for them to have sex tonight and she would probably regret it in the morning, so he would enjoy this night with her in his arms before they went their separate ways.

She murmured in her sleep and shifted closer to him, her soft, round behind pressing tighter against his groin. God, how could he not get carried away with . . .

Oh, fuck. He hadn't used protection. When she'd begged him to fuck her, his cock had been doing all the thinking. Not that that was an excuse.

He knew she was safe. He'd been tested since his latest, short relationship ended eight months ago. He was clean, and she probably was, too. He'd find that out later.

But what if she wasn't on birth control?

Kate awoke to the glint of sunshine. She opened her eyes and realized she didn't recognize the room she was in . . . and there was a hot, hard body pressed against the back of her, and big, strong arms around her.

Matt.

Oh, God, she'd had sex with Matt last night.

His breath against her temple was slow and steady. He was still asleep. She drew in a slow breath, then shifted forward slightly, trying to slip from his embrace, but his arms tightened around her.

"You know, you don't have to run away anymore." His deep voice rumbled from his chest, then his lips caressed her ear.

"I wasn't trying to run." It was actually a lie. If she'd been able to slip away, she would have dashed back to her room, gotten dressed, then pretended this had never happened. Now she had to face what they'd done head-on.

"You've been running from me for two years. I get it. It's a hard habit to break." He rolled her onto her back and smiled down at her, then captured her lips. Almost as soon as it started, the kiss was over. And she wanted more. "But now you know I'm not the frightening man you thought I was."

"Right." But he was. Not because he was the ruthless man Ileana had led Kate to believe he was, but because Kate knew that around him, she became someone else. That hadn't changed. Last night had proven that to her.

As he watched her, his brows furrowed. "Kate—"

"Look, Matt. Last night was a mistake. We should never have . . ." But it was her fault, not his. "I should never have asked you to . . ." Her hands clenched into fists. "Damn it. That's exactly why we can't do this. I beg you to dominate me, to punish me. Who does that?"

To her surprise, he grinned at her. "What's wrong with enjoying a little role-playing in the bedroom? It's healthy and it's exciting."

Her head shook back and forth. "But it's not a role. I become someone else. Someone I don't even recognize."

He drew in a deep breath and moved away, giving her much-needed space to breathe. "Okay, it's just as well. I didn't bring you here to start up a relationship again."

She gazed up at him. "Why did you bring me here?"

He'd drawn her here by saying he wanted to be an investor in her company and she prayed it wasn't just a ploy. She didn't want to let down her employees. Her heart clenched. And she didn't want to fail again.

"Kate, I didn't lie to you. I brought you here to discuss investing in your company."

"Really?" She was almost afraid to believe him. After the wild roller coaster of emotions she'd been through over the past twenty-four hours, she didn't think she could cope with another shock. "But . . . why? I mean, how did you even know I needed an investor?"

"A few months after you left me, I heard you'd moved away from New York and set up a business somewhere else. When I saw you at the mall recently, I wondered how you'd been doing. I asked around and found out you were looking for an investor." He shrugged. "I wanted to help."

"I realize you own Facts and Figures Inc., but what does the board of directors think about you investing in my company?"

"Actually, I'm investing personally. I thought you'd prefer that to being partners with a corporation." He shrugged. "I just made it look like they were the interested party because if you knew it was really me, I'm sure you wouldn't have agreed to come."

Her eyes narrowed. "You said you hadn't lied to me."

He grinned. "Well, not in any way that was important. So are you still interested?"

"Yes, of course."

"Good." He pushed away the covers and stood up.

She dragged her gaze from his nakedness. They were going to be discussing a business relationship. She shouldn't be drooling over his sexy, masculine body. Damn, how could she become partners with a man she'd been so intimate with? A man she'd drop to her knees for on command?

She drew in a breath, her fingers clenched around the sheets covering her. She'd find a way. Because she simply had to make this work.

He pulled on his pajama pants and turned to her. "So tell me, Kate, how are you?"

Actually, she felt incredibly refreshed. Once they'd made love, she'd fallen into a deep sleep, feeling warm and protected in his arms. Not that she would tell him that.

She gazed at his unsettling blue eyes. "I'm fine. A little hungry."

He grabbed something from his zippered bag and tossed it to her. A granola bar. "It's either that or leftover lasagna. I'd planned to have food delivered, but with the weather, that won't be possible."

"This is fine." She unwrapped it and took a bite.

"But what I meant is, how are you doing? Living here in Connecticut for the past two years?"

"Oh, it's a beautiful place to live. I have a nice apartment, friendly neighbors. I like to go biking in the fresh air. There are a lot of great parks and bike paths."

"So you like it here?"

"Yes, of course"—she gazed at the bar in her hand—"but I'd be lying if I said I didn't miss living in New York City."

The wistfulness of her words haunted Matt. She missed her old life. She never would have left the city if she'd had a choice. If circumstances hadn't forced her to move.

And he'd had a role in that.

"You have an apartment. You didn't want to buy a place?" he asked.

Pain lanced across her features. "No. I didn't want to fall in love with a place again and chance losing it. Maybe later, when things have settled down with my business."

She glanced at him, then down at her granola bar, and took a bite. The sadness in her eyes flooded him with guilt.

"What about you? Did you ever buy that big house you were looking at?"

"Yes, I did," he said, struggling to keep his voice emotionless. "I live there now." But he'd hoped one day Kate would live there with him. "From everything I've seen, your business is doing well. Why is your partner pulling out?"

———

Kate glanced at him in surprise. She was sure Matt would have found out all the details before he considered investing. "He got a great job offer in California."

"Yes, I understand the background. But even if he moves away, he could have kept his share in the business. Or was there something more than business between you?"

"No, he thought handling the business remotely would be too complicated. And the two of us were never involved. I know better than to mix a business partnership with romance."

Oh, damn. *How would he take that after last night?* She gazed at his inscrutable expression and decided she'd better tackle this head-on.

"Matt, about what happened last night—"

But his cell phone chimed from the dresser just as she started talking. She stopped while he took the call.

"Pearce," he answered. "Okay, good."

He hung up and tossed the phone on the bedside table.

"That was the driver. He said they should have the road cleared in an hour or so. He'll pick us up then." He grabbed his pajama top and pulled it on. "In the meantime, I think we're long overdue for some caffeine. We can take our coffee in the living room and sit by the fire. We have some things we need to talk about."

Her heart stopped at those words, but she nodded.

"I set the coffeemaker to start automatically, so it should be all ready. Are you coming?"

She was totally naked under the covers and was not about to hop out of the bed just yet.

"I'll meet you downstairs."

As soon as he left the room, she slipped from under the covers and dashed across the room, then peered out the doorway to see him disappear down the stairs. She hurried down the hall to her room and retrieved the robe he'd given her.

Matt walked into the kitchen and poured two cups of coffee, then walked through the door to the living room. Kate sat on the couch waiting for him. He sat down beside her.

"Matt, I'm sorry about last night."

"You're sorry?"

His stomach churned. Why was she sorry? Sure, he knew they couldn't really carry on their relationship, especially given certain facts he was not about to tell her, but he would never regret what happened between them last night.

"I'm sorry that things went too far, and I'm sorry if I hurt you. Back then . . . and now."

"You don't have to apologize. Especially about last night. There is, however, something important I need to ask you."

At his serious tone, she glanced up. "What is it?"

"Is it possible that you could be pregnant after last night?"

Shock vaulted through Kate. "What? No, why would you ask that?" Then she realized. "Oh, we didn't use a condom."

"That's right. I'm really sorry, Kate."

"I didn't even think about it. I mean, I know you. I trust you. It never even occurred to me that there'd be a problem. I mean, safety-wise." She glanced at him and noticed his tight expression had softened a little. "And I'm on birth control. I'm sorry, I should have told you."

Relief washed across his features. "Good. I wouldn't want a pregnancy to result from what we did last night."

Her stomach churned and she had to steady her breathing. As sensible as his statement was, it felt like a rejection. Of course he wouldn't want to be saddled with her and a bastard child just because of one night of indiscretion. Even though he had tons of money to spare, he wasn't the type of man who would just pay her off with child support. He was the kind of man who would want to be present for his son or daughter. And that would mean he'd be stuck with her, even if just for regular visits with their child.

Their child. The thought of having a child with Matt made her want to weep. Because she loved him and would love to have his child. But she and Matt just weren't right for each other. Oh, how she wished they were. He would be a wonderful father. And she would love to spend the rest of her life with him.

As she watched him take a sip of his coffee, her gaze slid along his square jaw covered in dark stubble, then down his pajama top to the solid, muscular chest peeking out. If only . . .

"I also want to apologize to you for what Ileana did to you," he said.

Anguish lanced through Kate at the memory of Ileana's lies, and the pain Ileana's friend had inflicted on her.

"But we've already established that you knew nothing about that."

"That's true, but I still feel responsible. I was the one who took you to that party." He shook his head. "I had no idea at the time that she was capable of such a thing."

"As you said"—her words sounded tenuous, but it was the best she could do—"you didn't know."

He nodded and sipped his coffee as silence hung between them.

"Before we begin our professional relationship, may I ask you something that's entirely inappropriate?"

She shrugged. "Well, given what happened last night, I suppose we're already on a roll."

He turned to her with a flicker of a smile. "Do you

think you can be truly happy in an ordinary relationship? Because I get the sense that you need a Dominant to bring out your true nature."

She shook her head. "I was—and am—totally uncomfortable with how we behave when we're together. In bed, I mean. I become so . . . submissive."

He raised an eyebrow and smiled. "And the problem is?"

"It's not me . . . normally. I'm only like that when I'm with you. And it's so . . . powerful . . . the need I have."

He gently lifted her hair from her face. "You can still be strong and independent, but be a sub in the bedroom."

"I know. I mean, theoretically I know, but when I beg you to punish me, I . . . ." She shrugged. "It's like I'm losing myself."

He stared at her for a long moment, the glimmer in his eyes unreadable. Then his mouth turned up in a lopsided grin. "So you don't like it when I punish you? When I bare your ass and discipline you? When I possess you in every way?"

Her insides fluttered at the thought, and heat wafted through her. As much as she resented the idea, it also turned her on. She *liked* Matt controlling her. *Dominating* her. "The problem is I like it too much."

Her mind slipped back to last night when his hand had smacked across her bottom as he'd punished her, then when he'd slid his fingers over her damp opening as he'd spanked her to orgasm.

The truth was, no one she'd ever been with had brought her the kind of pleasure Matt did. Every other lover was merely a pale comparison. He brought her senses to life in a way she'd never experienced before or after being with him.

Sitting before him like this and thinking about what they'd done last night made her painfully aware that she wore nothing underneath her robe.

She drew in a deep breath at the memory of his huge shaft thrusting into her again and again. Stretching her, driving deep. She longed to hold it in her hands. To taste it.

"Kate, when you look at me like that . . ." His blue eyes darkened.

She felt a growing hunger. And a deep need to be possessed by him.

He put down his cup on the table, and turned to her, his blazing eyes filled with just as much hunger as hers.

"Kate."

Her name on his lips made her long for him all the more. His hands wrapped around her face and he drew closer. He tipped up her chin and his lips devoured hers. His tongue thrust inside and his hand cupped her head, holding her to him, their mouths meshed firmly as he explored. She teased his tongue with the tip of hers, then they curled together. She glided forward, sliding into his mouth. Tasting black coffee.

All of her ached for him. She wanted him to take her so badly. But she drew back and gazed at him.

"Matt, I'm sorry. I don't know why I keep behaving this way."

He smiled. "It means we still can't keep our hands off each other. It means that we want each other so badly, it defies common sense."

She didn't know what she'd hoped for, but right now, knowing he wanted her as much as she wanted him was enough.

He captured her lips again, stealing her breath away. "Kate, I want you now."

She ached at his words.

"Me, too." She stroked down his hard, solid chest to his tight abs. When her hand stroked over his impressive bulge, he groaned.

His hands slid down her neck, then over her shoulders. He grabbed her robe and yanked it open.

"God, your breasts are so beautiful."

The awe and admiration in his eyes as he stared at her breasts sent delight wafting through her. His thumbs stroked over her nipples and they hardened instantly, sending tendrils of desire coiling through her.

———

Matt loved the feel of her breasts in his hands. So soft and round. The nipples hard under his thumbs. He leaned forward and licked one, then took it in his mouth and suckled lightly. She drew in a breath.

She was so turned on and that turned him on even more. His cock ached to be free of his constraining pants. She stroked him again and he swelled more. He eased her back on the couch until she lay beneath him, her breasts heaving with her labored breathing. He took the other nipple in his mouth and sucked.

"Oh, Sir, please—"

He covered her mouth with his, driving his tongue inside to stop her words.

He swirled his tongue in her mouth, deep and penetrating, until she was breathless, then he kissed down her neck, his tongue teasing the pulse point. He squeezed her breast, then leaned down and swallowed her hard nipple again. He swirled his tongue over the nub, again and again, then sucked deeply. At her gasp, he tugged again, then found her other nub and sucked until he elicited another gasp.

Her hand stroked the back of his head, then pulled him tighter as he continued to suckle.

"Oh, Matt, oh, yes."

She moaned and he could almost believe she'd orgasm right now if he kept going.

"Oh, Sir, please fuck me."

He kissed her again. "Kate, no 'Sirs' this time. We're just a man and a woman who want each other."

"Yes, Sir." She bit her lip. "I mean, Matt."

He smiled and captured her lips. His fingers burrowed inside her, and his thumb teased her clit.

"Do you like that, sweetheart?"

Of course, he could see it in her eyes. The glaze of desire as he tweaked her little button while his fingers stroked her slick opening.

"Oh, yes." Her words, drawn out and sexy, sent his desire skyrocketing.

Kate gasped as his hot mouth covered her nipple again. Intense sensations swamped her from all directions. His fingers gliding inside her. His thumb stimulating her clit, driving her pleasure higher. Then he sucked on her hard nub and she gasped. The sensations collided and she threw her head back and moaned as the sweet release swelled through her.

"Oh, yes. Oh, God." Her pelvis arched against his hand as she moaned loud and long.

He stroked and flicked, prolonging the feeling of euphoria as she floated on a plane of pure pleasure, her senses crackling like live wires as she quivered in bliss.

When she collapsed on the couch panting, his lips nuzzled her neck.

Joy bubbled from her in the form of a laugh.

He smiled down at her. "You enjoyed that."

"You know just what I like." She eased him back on the couch and slid to the floor in front of him, then stroked the bulge straining against the thin fabric of his pajamas. "And I know what you like."

She reached inside for the prize. Her fingers wrapped around his thick, swollen cock and she drew him out.

"Oh, God, you are truly enormous."

She could barely get her fingers around his thick, purple-tinged cock. It was hot and as hard as marble, with thick veins pulsing on the sides. It was so big that it was hard to believe it would fit inside her, but her core ached at the familiar sight of it, and the knowledge that he could drive into her and fling her to ecstasy.

She dragged her finger over the tip, loving that his whole body quivered at her action. A bead of moisture oozed from his small hole. She smiled and leaned forward, then lapped it up with the tip of her tongue. He groaned.

She knew he was close.

"Matt, I love to suck your cock, but I really want you to come inside me." She nibbled the edge of the corona with her lips, then dragged the tip of her tongue along it. "Do you think you can hold it?"

He nodded, with glazed eyes, then uttered a barely audible grunt as she widened her mouth around his cock-head, slowly taking it inside. She swept her tongue over the top, then closed her mouth and glided down the shaft. Just a little. Her hand still grasping the base of his cock glided downward, finding his balls. She stroked them, then cradled them in her palm.

"Oh, Kate."

His hard flesh tugged from her mouth and suddenly she was on her back on the couch, Matt above her. Hot flesh pressed against her slick opening, then Matt drove forward, his rock-solid cock filling her so deep she thought she'd die from sheer pleasure.

He pinned her arms over her head, then drew back and thrust deep again. His cock pulsed within her, sending shivers quivering through her.

She whimpered at the intensity of it.

He drew back very slowly, the ridge of his cockhead dragging along her inner walls, sending sparks fluttering through her.

"Oh, God. Oh, yes."

His lips found the pulse point at the base of her neck and the whisper-light touch combined with the iron grip on her wrists set her heart aquiver.

"Tell me how much you like me inside you."

"I love you inside me, Sir."

"You love it?" He grinned, stopping only halfway in. "Tell me more. I want to hear you talk dirty."

"I . . ." She sucked in air as he glided a little deeper,

then stopped. "Please, Sir, I love it when your big cock erupts inside me, filling me with your hot come."

He groaned and drove so deep she thought she'd die from the exquisite pleasure. Then he drew back and thrust again. Her insides quivered as she teetered on the edge of sanity. He drove in again and she gasped, pleasure trilling through her cells, dancing along her nerve endings.

"Oh, fuck." A guttural moan tore from his throat.

Then she felt it. Hot liquid pumping into her. She groaned, then pleasure erupted inside her, pummeling her with euphoria. He tightened his hold on her as she flung her head back and wailed her release.

His head jerked around. "Damn, what was that?"

But his words barely registered as she rode the wave of pleasure. He still pumped into her and she moaned as bliss crowned, then settled to a low, pulsing delight.

Then she heard it. A knocking sound.

Matt thrust a couple more times as her orgasm faded, then gently moved away from her.

"Kate, that'll be the driver at the door."

"What?" An adrenaline rush drove away the last traces of euphoria and she sat up. She could see the shadowy shape of the driver on the other side of the stained-glass door.

Damn, she'd assumed he'd call first.

"Don't worry about it," Matt said as he grabbed a phone from the stand on the end table. He dialed and held the phone to his ear. "Hi. I'm just finishing pack-ing. We'll be out in a few minutes."

Kate watched the shadowy figure on the other side of the door move away and sighed in relief, her heart still thundering in her chest. Then she scrambled up-stairs and began gathering her things. As she did, a deep sadness washed over her.

Would she just climb in that limo and head home, leaving this and Matt behind her? Of course, they'd be business partners, but as crazy as it seemed, she'd miss him terribly. Now that she'd rediscovered how amazing it felt to be with him, it was painful to think about go-ing on without him.

As she dressed, she realized she didn't have her pan-ties. Damn, they were still in Matt's room. She'd have to go get them. But first she went to the dresser and brushed her hair, then dabbed on some lip gloss. That's when she saw Matt in the mirror, standing behind her. She didn't turn, but met his gaze in the reflection.

There was a dark, haunted look in his eyes, and she imagined that he must be feeling the same sense of loss that she felt.

"Kate, there's something I haven't told you."

Matt crossed the room and sat on the edge of the bed, then folded his hands between his knees.

Kate turned. "But the driver . . ."

"He can wait." Matt stared at his hands. "I really should have told you this earlier."

She drew in a breath. "What is it?"

Matt's cell phone chimed. Annoyance flared through him as he pulled it from his pocket.

"What is it?" he asked sharply.

"Sir," the driver said over the phone, "city workers came by and informed me they're closing the road for repairs on some downed hydro lines. They said if we don't go now we'll be stuck here for a couple of hours."

"Fine. We'll be right down." Now he'd have to tell Kate in the car.

"What is it?" Kate asked.

"They're closing the road so we have to go right now. Ready?"

She nodded, quickly got her things, and followed him down the stairs. A few moments later, with full outerwear on to greet the cold morning, they went out the door. Matt took her arm as they walked down the steps, which were still icy, though the driver had scattered sand over the slick surface.

He met them at the bottom of the stairs and took Matt's suitcase, then opened the limo door for them. Matt helped Kate into the backseat.

Moments later, they were settled in the leather seats and the car was driving along the icy path she'd tried so hard to walk last night when all she'd wanted to do was escape from him. That all seemed so far away now. When she'd still believed he was a ruthless, terrifying man. Now, as she gazed at him, he saw trust in her eyes. And trepidation as she awaited his revelation.

When he revealed his secret, what would he see in her eyes then?

He pressed the button to close the smoked-glass barrier between them and the driver, giving them privacy. As soon as it closed, he drew in a deep breath and turned to her.

"Kate—"

Apprehension clouded her eyes and she rested her hand on his arm, her delicate touch stirring his heart.

"Wait, Matt. Let me say something first."

"Go ahead."

"About what happened this morning . . . and last night."

Now that they were leaving their quiet retreat, did she regret what they'd done?

"I think the fact that we wound up in bed twice in the space of twelve hours says something. I was wondering if you think . . ."—she gazed up at him, her wide eyes showing her deep vulnerability—"that maybe we have a chance. That we could try again."

He frowned. "You mean, a romantic relationship?"

Damn it, there was nothing he would love more, but . . . he couldn't. It would never work.

But how could he tell her that? Especially with hope shining so brightly in her eyes?

He took her hand in his. "We tried two years ago, and as much as we cared about each other, we knew deep inside that it really wasn't working." And it never would, especially after he owned up to what he'd done.

"I know that was largely my fault. I should have handled things better. I never intended to jump right into the Dom–sub stuff with you, but that first time when I asked you if you liked dominant men, you got so excited, and that excited me. I jumped into it right away. And you seemed to enjoy it so much. But I pushed you too fast and too far."

He drew in a deep breath. He should have talked to her about this long ago. Maybe if he had when they'd still been together, he could have done something about it. Maybe he could have salvaged their relationship.

She gazed at him with hope shining in her eyes. "I know I said I was apprehensive about my submissive nature with you, but maybe we can work it out. After losing you for two years, then finding you again . . . after feeling the magic we have together. I just think it's worth a try."

"No, Kate. Trust me, it just won't work."

From the disappointment in her eyes, he knew she

thought he just didn't want her anymore and he had to use iron will not to pull her into his arms. But that would be wrong. It would only hurt her in the end.

"Now, as I said, I have something to tell you. It has to do with Ileana."

The Arrangement

Kate steeled herself for what was to come. "What is it?"

"You know I met her because she'd done some legal work for a charity I'd been involved with. We had a few lunches together to talk about details and found we had some similar interests."

He'd told Kate a little about this before they'd gone to Ileana's party, so Kate knew he was referring to their common interest in the BDSM lifestyle.

"She and I became casual friends, and when she invited us to her party, I had thought it would be a great way for you to meet others in the lifestyle."

Kate nodded. "I remember."

"Yes, of course. The thing is, later it became clear that she wanted us to be more than friends. Since you and I were in a relationship, she must have seen this as an opportunity to get you out of the way."

Shock seeped through her. "Are you saying that she did what she did to scare me off?"

"I'm really sorry, Kate. I had no idea she'd do such a thing."

Her chest tightened. "So, did you date her?"

He sighed deeply. "Yes, briefly. After you and I broke up, she ensured she was conveniently around to console me." He squeezed her hand in his. "And I missed you so much."

Pain tore at his voice.

Kate's heart ached at the thought of Ileana holding Matt close, whispering soft words of comfort in his ear. Then that comfort turning to passion.

The thought of that witch taking Kate's man—pleasuring him and making love to him—made Kate ill.

Matt covered her hand with his, and the comforting warmth calmed her.

"I know you must hate me."

Her gaze darted to his face. "Hate you?" She rested her hand on his cheek. "Matt, I could never hate you."

As Matt gazed into her warm and loving eyes, he couldn't believe she was willing to forgive him for being with Illy after what the woman had done to Kate. He had expected to see hatred in her eyes.

He knew he should take this opportunity and tell her the rest, but he couldn't do it. He couldn't bear to see her trusting look wither and die completely. Not yet.

And it wouldn't be fair to her. Because at least now she would accept his financial help to get her company on track again. If he told her everything now, she would probably walk away. Or more likely run.

They sat in silence for a while, both wrapped in their own thoughts, as the miles passed them by.

"Kate, maybe we can't be together, but I want to help you. I really think that you could learn to accept your submissive nature, and I'd like to help you do that."

"What are you suggesting?"

He gazed deeply into her eyes. "You said you trust me."

She nodded. "I do."

"Then I have a proposal."

The car made a right turn, then curved around and came to a stop. Matt glanced out the car window and realized they were at the entrance to an apartment building.

"We're here, Mr. Pearce," the driver, whom they were still separated from by the glass barrier, said through the speaker.

Kate glanced out the window at the familiar front door to her apartment building. She wanted to hear what Matt had to say, and she really didn't want to say good-bye yet.

"Would you like to come up for a coffee?"

He smiled. "I'd like that."

The driver opened her door and she got out and stepped toward the entrance. Matt spoke to the driver for a moment, then followed her.

As they walked across the lobby, Ellen came through the door from the parking garage. She smiled when she saw Kate and hurried to join them at the elevator doors.

"Hi, Kate." Ellen smiled broadly and glanced toward Matt.

"Hi, Ellen. Matt, this is my friend and neighbor, Ellen."

Matt shook hands with her. "Nice to meet you."

The whole time Ellen beamed at him.

"Ellen, this is Matt. We used to know each other when I lived in New York." Kate knew Ellen was well aware this was Kate's ex. And from the broad grin on her face, she knew Ellen suspected they were getting together again.

If only it were true. Kate was disappointed that Matt had cut off that possibility so definitely. Yet he had some kind of proposal for her and she was dying to know what it was.

The elevator door whooshed open and the three of them stepped inside.

"So you're visiting from New York?" Ellen said. "Will you be in town long?"

"No, I'll be heading back this afternoon."

"Oh, that's too bad. It's a shame you and Kate couldn't spend more time together."

"We'll definitely be spending more time together since I'm hoping Kate will take me up on my offer to invest in her company."

"Really?" Ellen gazed at Kate with wide eyes. "That's wonderful."

"We're going to discuss it over coffee," Kate said, not wanting Ellen to get the wrong idea.

The elevator dinged as it stopped at Ellen's floor.

"Well, I hope it all works out." The door opened and Ellen stepped out, sending them a little wave as the doors closed.

"She seems nice," Matt said as the elevator continued moving.

"She is. She struck up a conversation with me when we were in the laundry room shortly after I moved here, and I guess she could tell I really needed a friend. She stepped into that role, and I'm glad she did. I appreciate her friendship and support. I know I can call on her anytime I need it."

"I'm glad you found someone in your time of need." His expression grew serious. "I wish I could have filled that role for you."

Kate shrugged. "If I'd still had you in my life, I never would have been starting out all alone in a new town."

She smiled. "I'm sure you would have let me stay with you for a while until I'd gotten back on my feet."

When the jobs had dried up, and the payments on her Manhattan apartment continued, she'd quickly realized that she had to make a change. She'd thought about renting another, more affordable apartment after she sold her place and staying in the city until she found something, but that would have left her in a precarious situation. When the opportunity in Connecticut had come up, she'd jumped at it. If she and Matt had still been dating, however, she knew he wouldn't have minded her staying with him while she worked things out. That would have given her the luxury of time before she'd had to make a move.

"Of course I would have." Matt's expression tightened with regret.

"It's okay. You couldn't help what happened."

Matt nodded, but it wasn't true. He hadn't known about the lies Ileana had told, or what had happened to Kate, but he did know why Kate had such trouble finding a job afterward, and he could have done something about it.

The elevator came to a stop.

"This is my floor," Kate said.

Matt followed her from the elevator and down the hall to her apartment door. As soon as he stepped inside, he knew this was Kate's place. Bookshelves lined the walls, full of colorful books of all types. She loved books: romance, mystery, DIY, decorating, art. She had very eclectic tastes in her decor, too. She had the same beige couches with bright floral cushions he remembered, along with what looked like a new glider rocker, and the large TV armoire her mother had given her. She used to read about feng shui and she'd told him once that a television should be hidden from view when not in use. For some reason, it was supposed to improve the energy of the room.

"Nice place," he said as he took off his shoes.

"Thanks. Not as ritzy as your penthouse, but it's home." She put her purse in the closet. "Come in. Would you like coffee?"

"Please." He walked into the living room and sat down on the couch.

He could hear Kate moving around in the kitchen and the clatter of cups and cutlery. He pulled out his cell and checked his e-mail while he waited. Nothing urgent, just an acknowledgment from his company lawyer that they'd get right on the contracts first thing Monday morning.

Kate returned a few moments later with a tray that held mugs, cream, sugar, and a coffee Thermos. She set it on the table and poured them both a cup, then put sugar and cream in hers. She knew he took his black.

Kate sat across from him on the rocker. "You said you had a proposal for me." She seemed anxious to hear what he had to say.

"Yes. Although I don't think you and I can be together, I do believe you'll eventually find a man who will make you happy and I think you'll have to face your discomfort, fear, whatever you want to call it, about being submissive. I believe if you meet the right man, and he handles things properly, I think you can be very happy."

She looked disappointed as she sipped her coffee. "That's not a proposal."

"True." He leaned forward. "What I propose is that I could help you to learn more about being a submissive so you can embrace that side of yourself."

She put down her mug and gazed at him with interest. "How would you do that?"

"I was thinking we could spend some time together, maybe a week or so, and I could train you. Sort of an intensive training course on how to be a submissive."

Her eyes grew keen with interest. "Train me how? I mean . . . would there be sex involved?"

"There doesn't have to be. I could teach you how to serve your Master, what kinds of things he might expect of you, how you should behave."

"But with no sex."

"It would be like learning the theory of flying before you actually go up in the plane."

She picked up her cup again and sipped. "But what if"—her fingertip circled around the rim of the cup—"I want to go up in the plane?"

At her words, and the sultry look she shot him, his cock swelled.

Could he really allow them to go this route even though there would be no romantic relationship between them? Then he thought about her calling him "Sir," and assuming submissive positions, and he wondered if he could survive *not* having sex with her.

"Wouldn't it make the experience more realistic? I'd learn better, wouldn't I?"

"Well, yes, that's true. If it's okay with you, and you understand it won't lead to anything else . . ." He sent her a questioning glance.

She nodded. "Yes, you've made that clear."

He gave a single nod. "Okay, then, you'll get the full experience."

"I'm curious what you'll be training me to do. Could you give me an example?"

"Certainly. Put down your cup and sit up straight," he said, slipping into his authoritative Dom voice.

She followed his instructions. As she sat up, her breasts thrust out more than when she was relaxed. He longed to tell her to take off her blouse so he could see those pert, naked breasts. But he wouldn't. Not here. Not now. Perhaps in the future, when he had her at his home. Then he would see her naked again, now that she'd opened the door for the sexual side to be part of their training. He could hardly wait to get her into the well-equipped dungeon he had and to chain her to the wall.

"Now it's very important that you address your Master with respect. You already know to call me 'Sir,' but sometimes you can call me 'Mr. Pearce.' Anytime you respond to me, you should use one or the other as a sign of respect. So what will you call me?" He knew asking questions was the best way to bring the lessons home.

"I will call you 'Sir,' Sir."

"Or?"

"I can also call you 'Mr. Pearce,' Sir."

"Good. Now I'd like you to mix it up and start using both terms."

"Yes, Mr. Pearce."

"Good girl." He rewarded her with a smile. "Now, many Doms will want their subs to take a certain position. Sometimes when they first see them, or sometimes when they give a certain signal. Sometimes the position is as simple as kneeling on the floor with their eyes cast downward. Sometimes it's something more sexual."

"Mr. Pearce, would you give me an example of the latter?"

Damn, she was being a real minx, but he loved her enthusiasm. "Stand up and move to the middle of the room."

She did so, but it was clear there wasn't enough space in her small living room.

"Move the coffee table out of the way."

She turned the rectangular coffee table ninety degrees, then pushed it against the chair, clearing enough room for what he had in mind. He grabbed one of the larger cushions from the arm of the couch and handed it to her.

"Now, turn around and get down on all fours."

Kate sank to the floor and knelt on her hands and knees.

"Put the pillow in front of you and rest your head on it, then lift your ass in the air."

She put her head on the pillow and, as instructed, pushed up her butt.

"Now, widen your knees."

He watched her try, but her skirt prevented it.

"My skirt's too tight, Sir."

"Hike it up."

She shimmied the fabric up her thighs and spread her knees wider.

"Now, usually you'd be naked and your Dom would want you to grab your ass cheeks and pull them wide, opening yourself to him."

"Yes, Mr. Pearce."

He almost gasped when Kate hiked her skirt up to her waist, revealing her totally naked ass. He hadn't meant it as a command. And, damn, he'd forgotten he still had her panties. His hand slid to his jacket pocket and slipped inside, finding the lacy garment there. He'd found them on the bedroom floor this morning and tucked them in his pocket to give them back to her, but with the rush to leave this morning, he had forgotten before they left the house.

Kate grasped her ass cheeks and drew them apart, revealing her intimate folds. They looked slick and ready for him. His cock pushed insistently at his pants. He wanted to kneel down behind her and glide right into her welcoming depths. Right now. He ached to do it.

"Now what, Sir?"

Thank God for the distraction.

"Now, you learn that you should remain quiet until your Master addresses you. He might want you to stay in this position for minutes, or even hours, at his pleasure. When you're like this, he might want to just stare at you. He might masturbate while he looks at you, or he might tell you to touch yourself."

"Like this, Mr. Pearce?"

She glided her fingers along her slit, then pressed them into her slick flesh.

"Stop," he said sharply. "You'll also need to learn discipline."

He stood up and walked toward her as she drew her fingers from her pussy and went back to holding her backside.

"Move your hands."

She let go of her delightful ass and rested her arms on the pillow, her elbows near her face. He placed his hand on her warm, round ass and stroked, then pulled back and smacked her cheek.

"What do you say now?" he demanded.

"I don't know, Sir."

"You say, 'Thank you.'"

He slapped her ass again.

"Thank you, Mr. Pearce."

He slapped her three times, catching her in mid "thank" with the second slap.

"When your Master slaps you several times, wait for the end. If there's a pause between slaps, then you can thank him. You'll get to know what your Master likes."

"Yes, Sir."

Her delightful ass, so red and round, called to him. His hand stroked over it and his cock twitched. He stroked her smooth flesh, then his fingers found her folds and glided over them. He could almost come on the spot at the feel of her slick, needy opening. His fingers pressed into her a little, then withdrew, then pressed in a little deeper.

A knock sounded at the door. He jerked his hand away.

"I hope that gives you an idea, Kate."

She lowered her ass and pushed herself to her feet.

Her cheeks glowed as red as her ass. She was clearly as turned on as he was. Of course, he already knew that.

"Thank you, Sir," she murmured, then pulled down her skirt and smoothed it with her hands.

Another knock. Kate hurried to the door. Damn the timing of whomever it was. Kate had been going crazy with need for Matt to touch her again, and when he started stroking her, pushing his fingers inside her, desire had swelled within her. Just a few minutes more and she was sure Matt would have driven his huge cock into her, and fucked her like crazy.

She peered through the peephole. It was Ellen holding a plate. Kate opened the door.

"Hi, I thought I'd bring over some brownies for you to have with your coffee." As soon as Ellen saw Kate's face, her eyes widened. "I hope I'm not interrupting anything."

"Not at all," Matt said as he headed for the door and grabbed his coat. "I really need to get going. Kate, I'll send over those papers on Monday and I'll call you about setting up that appointment we discussed."

He bent down to put on his shoes and tie them up.

"Do you really have to go now, Matt?" Kate asked.

He stood up. "Yes, I really have to get back." Then he disappeared down the hall.

"Oh, Kate, I'm sorry. I didn't realize that you were . . . Well, I thought it was just a business meeting."

"And why don't you think it was?"

"Well, first there's your face. It's flushed. And then there's the fact that I could see the edge of your lace panties in his suit jacket pocket."

Late Monday morning, Kate received the papers from Matt's lawyers. He definitely had an efficient team. Of course, knowing Matt, he'd probably already had the papers drawn up and just needed his lawyers to attend to the final details.

She looked them over. Everything was totally reasonable. After lunch, she took a walk and dropped the papers off with her lawyer, who had an office just a few blocks down from hers. He promised he'd look them over by the end of the day tomorrow and they'd meet to discuss them. She sent Matt an e-mail, telling him she'd be discussing the papers with her lawyer the next day.

That night, she dreamed of Matt. Touching her, commanding her. Making love to her. When she woke up, she masturbated to release the sexual tension thrumming through her.

God, she wanted him, and she was desolate that he didn't think they could make a go of a relationship, but she knew he was probably right. The relationship had been failing two years ago and it was unrealistic to believe it would be different now.

Why, then, did he want to teach her how to be

submissive? Would he do that in hopes of turning her around and making their relationship work?

Personally, she didn't think it would work. She liked being submissive. She liked it *too much*. That was the whole problem. The only reason she was doing this was because she wanted to be around Matt a little longer, in an intimate way. And she knew, if he was training her as a submissive, he wouldn't be able to keep his hands off her. That had been proven again and again.

So they might not be able to have a long-term romantic relationship, but they could continue a sexual relationship. For a little while, anyway.

The next morning, her lawyer called to set up an appointment for that afternoon, and they decided on four o' clock. She shot off an e-mail to Matt. After lunch, when she returned to her office, she checked her phone messages. There was one from Matt.

"Hi, Kate. I just wanted to let you know that I'll be in town this afternoon and will join you at your lawyer's office. That way, I'll be on hand to answer any questions or concerns, then we can sign the paperwork and get that out of the way. I'm hoping you'll join me for dinner afterward so we can discuss that other matter."

That other matter. The one where she became his slave for a week. Her breathing became labored at the thought.

As she walked down the street on the way to her lawyer's office, enjoying the bright sunshine and relatively mild temperature of the January day, a limousine pulled up beside her and the passenger window glided down.

"Kate? Want a ride?"

She glanced over to see Matt smiling at her. Her heart began to pitter-patter. The door opened and she stepped inside. She'd been enjoying the walk, but she enjoyed seeing Matt even more. Her knee brushed his as she sat down and heat pulsed through her.

The ride took only a minute since they were already so close. Matt accompanied her into the office and they pored over the papers together. Any issue her lawyer brought up, Matt responded to with ease, and on a few points, he approved changes to the wording to satisfy her lawyer. They were small enough that they just wrote the changes in, then both she and Matt signed the papers.

Matt held out his hand and she shook it. "Congratulations, partner."

His big hand encompassing hers felt good.

He opened his briefcase and pulled out a check, which he handed to her lawyer. It felt so official now. Matt was her partner. Shouldn't she feel nervous? Relieved? Maybe even panicky?

In truth, she felt all those things, but they were totally overshadowed by the sense of wonder she had just being near Matt . . . and knowing they'd be spending a leisurely dinner together, and maybe something more afterward.

Matt smiled as they exited the building and headed for the limo awaiting them on the street. "Now, I'm taking you out to a celebratory dinner."

They drove across town to an elegant little bistro she'd never been to before.

"So, Kate," he said after they'd ordered. "Have you thought about my other offer?"

Had she thought about it? She'd hardly thought about anything else. Hot images of him *training* her filled her days, and those images came to life in her dreams. They'd kept her at a sexual height for days. So much so that she could see herself sliding right under this table and devouring his cock rather than the delectable shrimp cocktail the waiter had just placed in front of her.

"Yes. As I mentioned before, I'm very interested." God, she couldn't believe her voice sounded so calm. As if she were talking about a business venture, when in reality they were talking about red-hot sizzling sex.

She took a sip of her ice water.

"I just wanted to make sure you hadn't started to reconsider."

"Not at all." She gazed at him with blazing eyes. "When?"

He smiled. "I was hoping we could spend a week

together." His eyes heated as he watched her bite into a plump, juicy shrimp. "I can clear my schedule anytime you like."

That surprised her, since Matt was a very busy man, with a huge corporation to manage. But then, he had a team of people to depend on. And Matt had always been able to set aside time for her. It seemed that hadn't changed.

She had also checked her schedule in anticipation of this request. Her team was actually just past the initial stages of their latest project and things were going smoothly.

"I could arrange to get away next week, or if that's too soon, maybe—"

"Next week would be perfect." His smile lit his face and she longed to grab his hand and drag him out to the limo where she would proceed to rip his clothes from his very broad, muscular body and devour him.

Over the rest of dinner, he talked about arrangements. The driver would pick her up at her apartment on Friday afternoon. He asked if she could get off a little early so she wouldn't lose the whole evening traveling. By the time they finished dinner, they had the details sorted out and he talked to her about running a business in a less hectic place than New York and how she had adapted. She carried her end of the conversation, but all she could really think about was what would happen when he dropped her off at her apartment. Would he come up for a drink?

Would he stay the night?

On the ride to her apartment, her heart thundered in anticipation and she couldn't help glancing at him from time to time, wondering what he was thinking. Their conversation had petered out and they rode mostly in silence. When the driver finally pulled up to her door, she turned to Matt.

"Would you like to come up for a drink?"

"No, I'm afraid not. I've got an early meeting in the morning."

Disappointment rocked through her, but he took her hand and kissed it, his warm lips brushing her skin. "But I look forward to seeing you Friday."

The driver opened her door, then saw her to the building entrance and opened the glass door for her, too. She glanced back at Matt and smiled, then proceeded into the building. Damn, she didn't know how she'd last until Friday.

Kate gazed out the car window at the huge mansion as the driver opened the door for her. He carried her bag up the steps and rang the doorbell.

Seconds later, Matt opened the large, oak door. She smiled at the sight of his strong, handsome face.

"Kate, so nice to see you."

The driver placed her bag inside the door, then took his leave. Matt closed the door behind him.

"Would you like some dinner?" he asked as he took her coat.

"No, I ate on the trip here."

There had been a selection of prepared food available in the limo: sandwiches, salads, a fruit plate, even pizza slices. She hadn't been particularly hungry—she'd been totally preoccupied with what would happen with Matt this evening—but she ate something anyway because she hadn't wanted to waste time with dinner once she got here.

He picked up her overnight bag and led her up the stairs to a large bedroom. She was disappointed when she realized it wasn't his. He set her bag on a bench by the window. There were no clothes in the bag because he'd told her to bring only the clothing she wore. He would be dictating what she wore this week as part of her training.

He pointed at items on the bed. "Put that on and leave your clothing folded outside the room, then meet me downstairs in ten minutes. On the dot. I'll be waiting for you in the living room."

"Yes, Sir."

Her insides tingled at the exchange. He was starting right into it.

He left the room and closed the door behind her. She gazed at the black leather items sitting atop the pristine white bedding. She walked over and lifted the boned corset, and realized it would not cover her breasts. She sifted through the items and did not see a bra.

She stripped off her clothing and folded up her suit and blouse, then wrapped the corset around her midsection and hooked it up. She found a leather thong and pulled it on, then stared at the four straps with buckles still lying on the bed. Finally, she realized they were ankle and wrist cuffs and she put them on. Finally, she put on the five-inch, steel-stiletto-heeled shoes.

She glanced at herself in the mirror and blanched at the sight. Was that really her? The corset pulled her waist in tight and the high heels made her legs look incredibly long. Her breasts, totally bare, seemed larger than usual in contrast to the tight black leather hugging her torso. Even more so with her hard nipples thrusting forward.

She crossed to the door, but as soon as she pulled it open, she realized she'd be walking through this big house half-naked. He probably had staff and someone might see her. She glanced at her watch and realized she had no time to think about it, since she had less than a minute until Matt's imposed deadline. She glanced around quickly before she laid her clothes outside the door, then she walked carefully down the stairs, gripping the banister tightly. She wasn't used to shoes this high.

———

Matt's breath caught as Kate stepped into the room, her naked breasts swaying as she walked. He was glad he'd given the staff the week off to leave them privacy, but he hadn't told Kate that yet.

"Good. Now, stand in front of me."

She walked toward him, then stopped a few feet in front of the armchair he sat in. He stood up. Then he stared at her breasts. Round, creamy, soft. As he watched, her nipples went from slightly hard to jutting straight forward, the aureoles pebbling. He longed to lean forward and take one into his mouth, then savor it as he stroked it with his tongue. Then he'd suck, slowly at first, then long and hard until she moaned in delight.

But that's not what this session was about. He wouldn't actually touch her this evening.

Slowly, he moved around her, scrutinizing her body. The contrast of her white skin with the black leather was seductive. The corset made her already small waist appear even smaller. The high cut of the thong paired with the extremely high, slender heels accentuated her long, shapely legs. And her ass, so round and firm, was completely exposed.

"Do you like me looking at you?"

She hesitated, and he knew she probably found it unnerving, because as beautiful as she was, she had doubts about her body and didn't like it being scrutinized too closely.

"Well?" he prompted.

"I'm not sure, Sir."

He suppressed a smile. Her desire to be touched was warring with her discomfort at being examined.

"Go and get the riding crop sitting on the table by the window."

She glanced around, then walked to the window and returned with the black leather stick and handed it to him. He took the handle and walked around her. He dragged the end of the crop over her shoulder, then down her arm. He glided it over her waist, then back up to brush the undersides of her breasts. She stood perfectly still, but he could sense a change in her breathing.

He walked behind her, and stroked her round ass with the stick. Then he drew it back and smacked it across her left cheek. Very lightly, but he knew it would smart a little. She gasped and the skin reddened a little.

"A good sub wants to please her Master at all times. That means, she likes what he likes. If he enjoys examining her body, she learns to enjoy it, too, because a Master's greatest pleasure is his sub enjoying his attention, and vice versa. Do you understand?"

He could tell she was a little confused. The truth was, he knew she enjoyed his looking at her; she simply had to push past her uncertainty. A good Master knew what his sub liked and would only push her when he knew it would enhance her pleasure.

He walked in front of her and was taken aback at the deep anxiety in her eyes.

"Kate, what's wrong?"

She stared at the floor, but he could feel the tension in her. "Nothing, Sir."

He tucked his hand under her chin and gently lifted her head until she was looking at him.

"Kate, step out of the role for a minute. Now tell me what's bothering you."

"I don't like the crop." Her voice was tight with tension.

"Okay, we'll put it away." He walked to the fireplace and put it down on the mantel, then turned. "Why didn't you tell me?" he asked, in a coaxing, encouraging tone as he walked back to her.

"I . . . didn't want you to think I don't trust you. I do, but . . ."

Damn, he was such a fool. "The whipping. I'm sorry, Kate. But remember that you can step out of the role anytime you want. You have control in these scenarios. Just like in the past, use your safe word."

Her face visibly relaxed.

"Do you remember your safe word?"

She nodded. "Triangle."

"Good." He smiled at her, then stroked her cheek and leaned in for a tender kiss.

Kate's anxiety diminished as soon as Matt put aside the crop, and now with the soft kiss, it drained away completely. As Matt's lips brushed hers, his hand cupping her face, she melted against him. His arm slid around her waist and he drew her tight to his strong, muscular body. She felt safe with him. She totally trusted him. The riding crop had just triggered memories that caused her insides to churn.

Now, with his strong arms around her, and her naked breasts crushed against his solid chest, heat wafted through her, and her nipples swelled. He was big and hard and masculine. He would command her to do things. To please him. And to please her. Her insides quivered.

He drew back and smiled at her, then his face returned to the dispassionate expression of her Master and he stepped back. He sat on his armchair again.

"Come here."

She stood in front of him and he gazed at her breasts, at his eye level. He continued staring. She felt the tingle of desire as they tightened and protruded straight out. He lifted his hands and stroked the sides of her breasts, then cupped them. Her nipples pushed into his palms and her insides coiled with need.

"You have lovely breasts."

"Thank you, Sir."

His thumbs stroked her nipples, sending sparks flittering through her. Then he took one nipple in his mouth and licked.

"Oh, Mr. Pearce. That feels so good."

He cupped her ass and drew her closer, then sucked hard. She gasped at the sharp, delightful sensation. He shifted to the other nipple and sucked it lightly. Too soon he released it, then eased her back a half step and gazed up at her.

"Now touch yourself. Show me what you like."

"Yes, Mr. Pearce." She touched her nipples, brushing them lightly with her fingertips. They were damp from his saliva.

"I want you to touch your pussy."

She glided one hand down her stomach, then over the leather crotch.

"Wait. Take off the thong."

She quickly disposed of the panties, then stroked over her folds. He watched intently as she glided between them to the moisture already pooled in her opening.

He caught her wrist and drew her hand from her dripping pussy, then took her index finger, glazed in her juices, into his mouth.

He licked it, then sucked. As he pulled it deep into his mouth, his wet, moist flesh pulsing around it, her core clenched in need.

He released her finger. "You're delicious. Now, kneel down and unzip me."

"Yes, Sir." She knelt in front of him, gazing at the big bulge in his pants.

She unfastened his button, then drew down his zipper, careful not to touch his bulge so she wouldn't be punished. Because punishment would delay her from putting her lips around that bad boy.

"Now reach in and pull out my cock."

She smiled. "Yes, Mr. Pearce."

She reached inside his boxers—a fine, silky cotton fabric—and wrapped her fingers around his big, wide shaft. It was so hot and hard, pulsing in her hand. She drew it from the fabric and admired it as it stood straight up, thick and solid.

She wanted to lean in right now and glide her lips along his length. To have him erupt in her mouth and swallow all he gave her.

"You don't need to respond with every command. Okay?"

"Yes, Sir."

"Good. Now, take off your clothes."

Reluctantly, she released his big cock and stood up. She unfastened the hooks down the side of her corset and peeled the leather away, then tossed it aside. She shivered in excitement as she stood there totally naked, except for her shoes and the leather cuffs, and he sat fully clothed, but with his huge, throbbing cock pushing from his pants, at full attention.

"Go sit on the chair across from me."

She had to stop the "Yes, Sir" that leaped to her tongue. She walked the few feet to the other chair, then turned and sat down.

"Open your legs so I can see you."

She sat with her knees wide apart and quivered in need as he stared at her most intimate parts.

"Touch yourself. Give me a sexy show."

She stroked one nipple with her fingertips while she slid her other hand to her soft folds. While her nipple throbbed between her pinching fingers, she stroked her slick flesh, then glided a finger inside her hot, wet opening.

"Are you wet?" he asked.

"Yes, Mr. Pearce. Very wet."

She stroked over her clit and her insides clenched.

"Are you touching your clit now?"

"Yes, Sir."

She vibrated her fingers over it lightly, watching him as his big hand wrapped around his cock and squeezed.

"It feels so good, Sir."

"Are you getting close?"

She vibrated faster. Pleasure rose within her.

"Oh, yes, Sir."

"Keep stroking that sweet little clit."

She stroked harder, feeling the pleasure build. It wouldn't be long.

"But I don't want you to come."

Oh, damn. She arched against her hand, so close she could barely stop it.

"But I'm so close, Sir."

"Stop."

Damn it! She stopped touching herself, need burning through her like a branding iron.

"Come over here."

She walked to him.

"Kneel in front of me and lick my cockhead."

She knelt in front of him and gazed at his huge cock. She leaned forward and licked the tip, tasting the salty pre-come. He was rock hard for her.

"Hold it and suck it."

She wrapped her hand around the thick, throbbing shaft and drew it to her lips, then swallowed him inside. His huge mushroom-shaped head filled her mouth. She sucked, and glided down, taking half of him, then she slid back again. Sucking harder, she glided down again, then back.

"Okay, stop."

Slowly, she released him. He stood up, drawing her to her feet, too. Then he turned her around.

"Sit."

She sat on his chair, still warm from his body. He knelt in front of her and pressed her knees wide apart, then leaned forward. She gasped as he licked her sensitized clit. Two thick fingers glided inside her and she clenched around them.

"You are so fucking wet."

He sucked on her clit and she gasped again, her head falling against the back of the chair as she arched against his mouth. His tongue teased her mercilessly, then he sucked again. Pleasure shot through her, then waves of ecstasy erupted within her. Pulsing. Washing through every cell.

She moaned as he continued to suck and lick, his fingers thrusting in and out.

"Oh, Mr. Pearce. I'm—" She gasped again as he sucked hard. "I'm coming."

She wailed her release, her fingers coiled tightly in his dark wavy hair.

"Sir, please fuck me now."

He kissed her clit, then leaned forward and licked her nipple, then gave it a quick suck.

"I was going to just ease into things tonight. No actual fucking." He smiled. "But you have been such a good little sub."

He took her hands and drew her to her feet, then guided her behind the chair and pressed her forward against the back of it. Standing behind her, he stroked her long hair from her neck and nuzzled, sending tingles through her. His big body leaned against her, his hard cock throbbing against her back. She longed for that big cock to be inside her as he swept her hair from her back and tossed it over her shoulder, then nuzzled her neck again.

He wrapped his hand around his cock and guided her until she was bent over the chair back, his mouth still playing over her neck. His cock glided between her legs, stroking her slick folds. Her vagina clenched as she anticipated the invasion of his pulsing, rock-hard member. His lips slipped from her neck as his shaft stroked over her folds again. Oh, God, she was desperate for him inside her.

"What the hell?" he exclaimed.

To her utter disappointment, his cock fell away and his hot body shifted. His finger stroked down her back.

"Kate, these scars . . ."

She tensed as he drew her to her feet and turned her to face him.

Matt had been just about to drive into Kate's sweet wetness when he'd seen a series of angry red scars on her back. Now she stared at him with wide, vulnerable eyes.

"Were these from that night? That guy?"

She nodded.

"Oh, fuck, I'm so sorry, sweetheart. I had no idea . . ."

She'd told him the guy had whipped her, and he'd heard her screaming in her dreams, but he'd still had no idea how bad it had been. To leave scars like that . . . Fuck.

He tugged her into his arms and held her close, stroking her hair. "I wish I had been there to protect you."

"It's okay. I'm okay," she said.

"No, it's not okay." Fuck, he wanted to kill the guy who'd done this to her. He wanted to keep her in his arms forever and protect her from the world.

"I've been such an idiot. Punishing you after what you went through. Kate, fuck, I was such an insensitive ass to bring out the riding crop tonight."

"No, Matt." She stroked his cheek, gazing at him with wide eyes. "You spanked me that first time because I asked you to, then later because you knew how much I liked it. And tonight, you could tell I was nervous and you asked me about it. Then you put it away." She kissed him softly. "I know I can trust you."

He captured her lips again, possessing her mouth with passion. "Of course you can trust me. I love you."

He swept her into his arms and carried her up the stairs and into his bedroom. He placed her on the big bed and prowled over her.

She smiled up at him. "Oh, please, Mr. Pearce." Her delicate fingers wrapped around his aching cock. It twitched in her hand, pulsing with need. "I want you to fuck me."

She pressed his cockhead to her wet folds, and he

glided inside her, unable to stop himself. Fuck, she was so hot and wet. He groaned as she tightened around him in an intimate hug.

"Oh, God, Kate, I want you so much."

He drove deep and she moaned.

Kate almost fainted at the intense pleasure of his huge cock filling her to the hilt. "Oh, yes, Sir. Please fuck me hard."

She was still elated at his proclamation of love.

He drew back and drove deep again. His lips nuzzled her neck as he drew back. Then he glided forward. She wrapped her legs around his waist, opening wider for him. This time his cock filled her even deeper.

Pleasure rocked through her and she moaned. Soaring higher as he thrust again and again. His body pounded against her, filling her with his hot marble shaft over and over. She groaned as sweet bliss spilled through her, then erupted into a cataclysmic orgasm.

She hugged him tight to her. "Oh, Matt. Oh, yes." Then she wailed so loudly, she feared she'd wake the neighborhood. He ground against her and grunted, spilling inside her in a wash of heat.

Then her consciousness shattered and she rode the wave of ecstasy.

Finally, she fell against the pillows, gasping for air.

He nuzzled her neck and she smiled up at him.

"So you love me," she said coyly.

As soon as she said it, she regretted it. The light in his eyes flickered and went out, then he drew back. His cock slipped from inside her and she felt empty. Physically and emotionally.

"Kate, I'm sorry, I should never have said that. I meant it when I said I would never hurt you, but . . ." He shook his head and drew away from her.

Her heart pounded, but she drew in a deep breath. "Okay, I get it. I'm pretty tired." She pushed herself from the bed and walked toward the door. "I'll see you in the morning."

She waited for him to protest, but he didn't. She would love nothing better than to curl up against him and sleep in his arms, but instead, she walked down the hallway to the guest room. She kicked off her high-heeled shoes, stripped off the ankle and wrist cuffs, and glanced around. She had no nightgown or pajamas, so she climbed into bed naked.

Matt threw his arm over his head on the pillow and stared at the ceiling, glowing in the soft illumination of the moon. He wished things had gone differently two years ago. That he and Kate hadn't slipped apart.

That Ileana hadn't ruined everything. That party showed there was a wedge between him and Kate that he hadn't really known existed. The pain he'd suffered because of Kate walking out on him had been intense, ripping his heart to shreds. All because of Ileana.

And then, after Kate had gone and Matt was suffering from a broken heart . . . He would love to blame Ileana for what happened, and she had certainly played her part, but he had to take responsibility for his own actions. He was the one who had ultimately betrayed Kate.

He rolled over again. All he could do now was to try and help Kate find her future happiness. The question was, would she even stay for the rest of the week?

Kate walked into the huge tile and glass shower in the guest room's en suite bathroom and turned on the water, then leaned into the warm spray. Matt had texted her a few moments ago, telling her he'd left some clothes outside her bedroom door and asking when she'd like breakfast.

In the shower, she pressed the shampoo dispenser on the wall and lathered up her hair. He was being sensitive, giving her a little more time before she had to face him, knowing it would be awkward after him saying he loved her, then taking it back.

She thought about the clothes Matt had left for her. At the door, she had found a bag with a thick, fluffy robe, and a pair of jeans with a cozy sweater. The latter was not exactly what she'd imagined he'd like her to wear during their week of sex, especially hot Dom-sub sex.

She rinsed the lather from her hair, then reached for the other dispenser and pumped body gel onto her palm. It smelled like magnolia blossoms. She stroked the gel vigorously over her body. Normally, she'd delight in the rich lather and the exotic scent, but right now she was too distracted.

Did Matt want her to leave? He might find it uncomfortable being around her now. Or was he just making it easier on her if she wanted to go?

She glided her hands over her breasts, swirling over the nipples. Their next encounter was bound to be awkward, but she really didn't want to give up a week with Matt. Her nipples puckered as she thought of Matt's big, muscular body. She wished he was here right now, scrubbing her clean, stroking over her naked body. She glided her hand down her belly and between her legs. The slickness there was not just soap.

Thoughts of his big cock, gliding into her, filling her more than her fingers ever could, sent her hormones into overdrive. Within seconds she was leaning against the tiled wall, shuddering her release, while the shower water still poured over her.

As Kate walked into the kitchen, Matt looked her up and down and she'd knew he was assessing the fact that she wore the robe he'd left for her rather than the sweater and jeans.

"Good morning," she said.

"Good morning. Why don't you sit down and I'll pour you a coffee. Breakfast is almost ready."

He stood up to get the coffee, then returned to the table with the pot and filled her cup.

"About last night . . . ," Kate said as he sat down at the table. She knew Matt and she could tell he was going to try to push her away. She decided to address the issue head-on.

Matt raised his eyebrows.

"When you said you loved me, it threw us both off a little," she continued. "But that doesn't mean we have to end this week together."

His gaze shot to hers.

"You *were* going to ask me to leave, right?" Her lips compressed. "The jeans and sweater you gave me to wear are far from sexy attire for a submissive."

"I thought you'd want to leave."

"Matt, you told me before we came here that you weren't interested in rekindling the romance between us. I knew that coming here. I realize that last night we both got caught up in being together again. We remembered how we felt in the past." She stared into his dark blue eyes. "But I realize that's all it was."

At least for him.

She stood up, and stepped toward him. "I don't want

to leave." She stroked his hair, loving the feel of the waves under her fingertips. "I want to make this week work."

He grasped her hand and held it. "Kate, if you're hoping I'll fall in love with you . . . if you think you're in love with me . . ."

She shook her head. "I know that's in the past. We won't talk of love again, except to say"—she smiled and drew her hand from his, then leaned close and pressed her face near his ear, his dark hair caressing her cheek—"I love being with you."

She untied her robe and let it fall open, then pushed the table back and stood in front of him. His gaze dropped to the narrow opening over her chest, locking on the visible swell of her breasts. She took his hand and guided it under the fabric, then pressed it to her naked breast.

Settling on his thighs, facing him, she stroked over the bulge in his jeans. "And I love having sex with you."

Matt seemed thoroughly mesmerized by her words and actions. She tugged down the zipper of his jeans, then wrapped her fingers around his twitching cock.

"And I really love having your big cock inside me." Her lips danced along his angular jawline.

When she started to glide downward, he curled his fingers behind her head and cupped it, then drew her forward. His mouth matched with hers and he thrust his tongue into her depths. She opened, allowing him to possess her mouth. He stroked, caressing every surface. His tongue tangled with hers and they undulated together in a passionate rhythm. When he released her mouth, she gasped for air.

"Now, kneel down," he demanded, slipping her hand from his cock.

She smiled and crouched down, gazing at his enormous cockhead peering out of his jeans, Matt's hand firmly around it. He brushed the head against her lips and she opened. His cockhead glided into her. She wrapped her lips around him as the corona filled her mouth. She sucked on him, loving the feel of him filling her.

Slowly, he moved forward, pushing his cock inside her. She sucked and squeezed as he glided deeper. He filled her mouth and her throat.

He groaned. "God, you feel so good around me."

She sighed at the delight of giving him pleasure.

He reached down to her face and stroked her cheek.

He thrust into her mouth, as if making love to her. In and out. Pleasure washed through her, then he groaned and jerked deep. Hot liquid flooded her. More and more. Filling her with heat, and lust for more.

When he finally pulled his cock from her mouth, she cried out, "Oh, God, Sir, please fuck me." Her insides churned in need. She had to have him now.

He drew her to her feet and backed her against the

wall. She clung to his shoulders as he pressed his big cockhead to her dripping wet opening.

His lips trailed along her jawline, sending heat simmering though her. "I'm going to fuck you now. Fill you so deep . . ." He nipped her neck. "Possess you so fully, that you will have no doubt I am your Master."

"Oh, yes, Sir," she pleaded. "Fuck me."

His cock drove into her, filling her deeply. His cock was long and thick. He stretched her beyond belief. Pleasure rippled through her, filling her entire being.

She wrapped her arms around him. "Make me come, Mr. Pearce."

He drove into her. Again and again. Mercilessly.

Filling her with such intense pleasure she thought she'd explode.

"Oh, yes."

The nerve-tingling sensations of his big cock filling her, his hard body ramming her against the wall, his lips pressing against her temple, all combined to drive her to a level of bliss beyond the mere physical world.

She gasped as his cock drove deeper still, then she wailed, clinging to his shoulders. Every nerve ending burst with pleasure and she surrendered to their shared ecstasy.

The doorbell rang and Kate put down the newspaper and glanced toward the door. Should she get it? Matt had told her there was no staff on duty this week and he had apologetically gone to the office for an hour or so, despite it being Saturday, because his assistant had called with some kind of emergency that couldn't wait until after Matt's week off.

The doorbell rang again. She decided she might as well answer it. She went and opened the door. Her heart stammered when she found herself face-to-face with Ileana.

"What are you doing here?" Kate demanded.

Ileana pushed past her and waltzed into the house. "I think the better question is, what are you doing here?"

Kate's eyes narrowed as she followed the woman into the kitchen. Ileana opened the fridge and helped herself to one of the blue glass bottles of imported water Matt kept chilling in the door, then grabbed a glass from the cupboard without skipping a beat. Clearly the woman knew her way around the house.

"I know that everything you told me about what happened at the party was a lie," Kate said. "Matt had nothing to do with that man."

Ileana smiled at Kate as if she were genuinely amused. "Well, aren't you the little genius? Too bad you figured it out eons too late."

Ileana strode into the living room as if she owned the place. Kate followed her, feeling a little like a pet dog trotting after its master.

"So, have you seen his dungeon yet?" Ileana asked casually. "It's *much* more elaborate than mine."

Kate remembered the harsh feel of Ileana's dungeon, with chains hanging from a cold brick wall and a selection of whips and floggers displayed on a wooden table.

She wanted this woman to leave. Just having this treacherous person here sent shivers down her spine.

Ileana switched the radio station from the soft music Kate had on to a hard rock station. "It's in the basement and well soundproofed." She glanced at Kate with a wicked smile. "No one would hear you scream."

Ignoring the queasy feeling in the pit of her stomach, Kate planted her hands on her hips. "I know what you're trying to do and it's not going to work. You drove Matt and me apart before, and I won't let you do it again."

"Did you know Matt and I were a couple?"

"He told me you dated briefly, but it didn't mean anything."

Ileana nodded. "I see. That's what he told you."

Kate crossed her arms. "That's right."

Her eyebrow flicked upward. "So why did he propose to me then?"

Kate's breath caught, but she knew it was a lie. "I don't believe you."

Ileana's lips turned up in a predatory smile. "I know you don't." She reached into her shoulder bag and pulled out an iPad, then flipped it on. "But I have proof."

After a few touches of her finger on the screen, she turned the device to face Kate.

Shock careened through her as she stared at a picture of Ileana and Matt together, Matt slipping a huge diamond ring on her finger, Ileana beaming like . . . well, like a woman who'd just been proposed to.

Kate glanced up at the woman's smirking face.

"There's *a lot* you don't know about Matt. Shall I fill you in?"

The Submission

Kate's blood froze. Matt had told her Ileana had meant nothing to him. That he'd only dated her for a short time, then ended it when he realized how manipulative she was. Now she was staring at proof that he'd been lying.

Ileana flicked her finger across the iPad to display other pictures of her and Matt while they shopped for a ring, the two of them smiling and laughing, just like any newly engaged couple would while searching for the perfect symbol of their love.

Kate felt ill.

"Everything was great between me and Matt until he saw you running through some shopping mall a couple of weeks ago." She said it with distaste, as if she wouldn't be caught dead in a mall. "Then he decided he wanted to go after you again."

Ileana turned off the iPad and slid it back into her purse. "He told me he just wanted a quick fling with you. Since I know how much he's always wanted to train you into total submission, he hoped I'd be understanding enough to indulge him." She shrugged. "I'm pretty open-minded. I don't mind swapping partners, and definitely threesomes are great, but . . ." Her sharp gaze locked onto Kate. "I draw the line at an obsession like you. I told him he had to choose. You or me."

"And he chose me," Kate said, but found no pleasure in it.

Ileana took a sip of her water, then nodded. "But don't get too excited about it. I know Matt and he knows me. He figures he'll have his fun with you, then when it's over, he'll come chasing after me again, assuming he'll be able to win me back." She smiled. "And ordinarily he'd be right. But this time, I've decided not to let him have his way. So I'm leaving for good."

"Is that why you came here? To tell me he's all mine now?" Kate said with sarcasm, wondering what was really at the heart of this woman's visit.

She just laughed. "Don't kid yourself. You won't be able to hold on to him any more than I could. He's an incredibly screwed-up guy and he's incapable of a normal relationship." She put her glass down and paced across the room. "No, I'm here because I made a mistake. I gave him back his ring and now I'm having second thoughts."

Kate frowned. "So you want him back?"

Ileana laughed. "No, I don't want *him* back. I want the ring."

"Oh." The word escaped from Kate's lips, as she wondered how Ileana could possibly let Matt slip away if she had a choice. "Why?"

Ileana shrugged. "I'm moving to L.A. Making a new start. That ring will go a long way to a down payment on a condo. I think I deserve that." She walked toward the stairs. "So I'll just go get it and get out of your hair."

Kate stepped in front of her. "I think not." Kate was not about to let Ileana, or anyone else, take something from Matt's house without his permission.

"It's my ring." Ileana glared at her.

"Not once you gave it back to him. If you want it, you'll have to ask Matt for it."

Ileana turned thoughtful. "I would think you'd help a girl out. After all, he betrayed you, too."

"I told you, I don't believe Matt was in on that horrible incident you arranged at the party."

Ileana's lips turned up in a condescending smile. "I wasn't talking about that, sweetie. I bet he didn't tell you that—"

A beeping indicated that Kate had received a text. She pulled the phone from her jeans pocket and glanced at it.

"Matt will be here in a few minutes," Kate said.

"Well, that will be awkward. Look, why don't you just be a dear and run up and get the ring for me? Then I'll be out of here and you can return to whatever little games you and Matt have been playing. The ring's in his bedside table. The one nearest the window."

"I said no." Kate's head was swirling with confusing thoughts and emotions, and she wasn't sure what to believe, but there was one thing she was certain of: Ileana would not leave here with anything she didn't have when she'd arrived.

Except my peace of mind.

Ileana's eyes narrowed, but she drew her shoulders back, then turned and marched out, slamming the front door behind her.

Kate drew a sigh of relief, but one thing kept nagging at her. What else hadn't Matt told her?

Kate glanced at her watch. Matt actually said he'd be back in about an hour, but she'd wanted Ileana out of here. She had hoped that telling her Matt would arrive imminently would hasten her exit.

She gripped the banister and slowly walked up the stairs. Step by step. Heading toward Matt's room at the end of the hall. She pushed open the door, then walked toward the bed, staring at the bedside table as if it were Pandora's box.

Which to her it was.

If she opened that drawer and found an engagement ring, it would not only back up Ileana's story about him giving her a ring—which was already pretty clear from the pictures—but it would prove that Matt still had feelings for Ileana. Otherwise, why would he keep the ring? And so handy.

Did he pull it out and stare at it, wondering if he had made the wrong choice chasing after Kate? Did his heart really belong to Ileana?

She sank onto the bed. Had Matt really come after Kate—offered to invest in her company and all—just to engineer things to get her here for this week of domination? She stared at the closed drawer. For Matt, the money was pocket change, so it was possible.

At a noise from downstairs, her gaze darted to the doorway. Had that been the lock on the front door unlatching? She grabbed her cell phone from her pocket and stared at it. Oh, God, Matt had texted her again, saying that he'd been able to get away earlier than he thought and he'd be home in five minutes. That was five minutes ago. She had been so caught up in her emotional turmoil, it hadn't registered.

The door opened, then closed.

What would she do? He expected her to be ready for their next lesson. When he'd been called to the office this morning, efficient Matt had decided to use this as an opportunity. A Dom would expect his obedient submissive to be ready and waiting for him.

Part of her wanted to march down the stairs and confront him about his relationship with Ileana, and the ring. But what was the point? She didn't own him. She wasn't even in a relationship with him. And he'd made it clear this wouldn't lead to a relationship.

She could hear him on the stairs and her heart thundered in her chest.

The only thing she could reasonably be angry about was that he'd lied to her about his relationship with Ileana, but maybe he'd done that to spare her feelings. Or maybe Ileana had lied to her, despite the pictures.

Okay, she needed time to think. She wasn't ready to confront Matt about any of this right now. Especially after what had happened last night.

She heard Matt's footsteps on the hardwood floor of the hallway.

It would be easier to continue with their plans, then gather her wits later. She would confront Matt about these things then.

But what would she do right now? She glanced around the room in a panic. She didn't have time to don the leather outfit he'd given her. It was in her room anyway. And he'd be here in seconds.

What would a good sub do?

She began tugging off her clothes, thrusting the pieces under the bed, out of sight, then she stripped off her bra.

His footsteps drew closer.

She whipped off her panties and threw them and the bra out of sight as well, then climbed on the bed and did the only thing she could think of. She got into the position he had taught her in her apartment when she'd asked him to explain about the training.

She knelt and placed her head on the bed, widened her knees, and lifted her ass in the air, her back end toward the doorway.

Matt walked into the room and his breath caught as he saw Kate's naked ass hiked up in the air, her knees wide and her intimate folds on display. His gaze locked on her shaven pussy, and his cock lurched to attention.

"Hello, Kate."

"Hello, Mr. Pearce." Her voice was a little muffled with her head turned sideways and her cheek pressed against the duvet.

"You're not wearing the outfit I instructed you to wear."

"Sorry, Sir. I didn't time things properly, and I didn't want to keep you waiting. I hoped this would please you."

He walked closer to the bed, a smile turning up his lips as he took in the graceful line of her naked body folded on the bed. With her chest pressed tight against the duvet, her breasts were hidden from view. He'd bet her nipples were hard.

He stroked his hand over the curve of her creamy derriere, enjoying the feel of her smooth, silken skin.

"Yes, I like seeing you on display like this very much, but you must learn to follow my commands to the letter."

He lifted his hand and smacked her bare ass.

"Right?" He smacked again, a little harder this time.

"Yes, Mr. Pearce," she said breathlessly.

He caressed her slightly reddened ass a few more times, gazing at her exposed folds. They glistened in the light. He glided his fingertips over her slit and almost groaned at the feel of her slickness. He slid his fingers into her, stroking deep inside her passage. He slid his thumb over her clit, loving the catch in her breath.

She was dripping wet now. He drew in a breath and pulled from her sweet heat, then crossed to his dresser and opened one of the side drawers. He found the silicone device and returned to her. He pressed the head of the small plastic cock to her opening and pressed it inside. He pushed it in and out a couple of times, until it was thoroughly coated in her slickness, which would act as a natural lubricant, then he positioned it against her back opening.

She stiffened as he pressed it slowly forward.

"Relax. Just let it go in."

They had shared anal sex in the past, so he knew this wouldn't be too challenging for her, but he eased it in slowly. Once it was all the way in, the flat, round end rested against her cheeks, preventing it from being drawn further into her body.

"Good. Now sit up."

She lowered her ass and pushed herself up, then turned and sat on the end of the bed. As his eyes feasted on her beautiful breasts, tipped with hard, tight nipples, his cock ached at the thought of the butt plug nestled tightly in her ass.

He stepped in front of her. "Now, suck my cock."

"Yes, Mr. Pearce." She unfastened his zipper, the delicate touch of her fingertips moving over his crotch causing his cock to twitch in excitement. She wrapped her warm fingers around him and drew him out.

He almost groaned as her lips surrounded him. She took him deep, then slid back, then glided forward again, taking him deeper each time, until he was fully immersed in her. He forked his fingers through her long auburn hair and guided her head forward and back. He resisted the urge to thrust into her mouth, just letting her do the work. She glided her hand under his balls and cupped them gently, then fondled them.

"Fuck, that feels good." His cock ached with the need to release. "Make me come, Kate. I want to fill your mouth."

She glided faster, tightening her lips around his shaft as she took him deep into her heat. Squeezing him as she moved.

"Oh, yeah." Heat flared through him. "Come on, baby. I'm so close."

Then pleasure speared through him and he erupted into her mouth.

Kate felt his cock release, filling her mouth with hot liquid. She swallowed, then glided off his deflating cock. She sat back and the butt plug shifted a little inside her, reminding her of its presence. She gazed at him, so hot she wanted him to flip her over and drive into her right now. The thought of his big, thick cock gliding into her sex while the butt plug filled her ass had her close to swooning. It would be like having two men inside her at the same time.

"Go and put on the outfit I gave you to wear. Meet me in the kitchen in ten minutes."

"Yes, Sir."

She stood up and hurried out the door to her room. It would take almost that long to put on the tiny garment, or at least to figure it out with all the straps. She picked it up and tried to figure out what went where. She fastened a strap around her waist, then another behind her neck. The straps surrounded her breasts and crisscrossed her body. Next, she slipped on the tiny leather thong. She glanced in the mirror. The black straps against her pale skin looked very striking. And sexy, with her breasts totally naked and her nipples poking forward at full attention. Four short straps still lay on the bed. Wrist and ankle bands. She sat on the bed and began fastening each into position.

She knew she should be thinking about Matt's lie about his relationship with Ileana. She knew she should consider walking away from this week with him. But she didn't want to. Maybe she couldn't trust him in the relationship department, but he wasn't offering her a relationship . . . other than business. But this week . . . Oh, God, as soon as he'd walked into the room, she'd started getting wet. His masculine presence dominated any room, and she was helpless to resist him.

She finished fastening the second ankle strap and glanced at the clock, then shot to her feet as she realized she had less than a minute to get downstairs. She grabbed the high-heeled pumps with the metal stiletto heels that he'd given her with the outfit and hurried down the hall, knowing she'd move faster carrying them than wearing them. Once at the bottom of the stairs, she stepped into them, then continued to the kitchen.

"Late again." He stood in the kitchen, a command-ing male specimen, even when totally naked.

Especially naked. His big cock hung in front of him like a pendulum, then it began to stiffen as his gaze glided the length of her. When it rested on her naked breasts, her nipples puckered. Oh, God, she wanted him to touch them.

"You really need to learn some discipline. And I have just the solution. Follow me."

He walked out of the kitchen and down the hall, Kate following on his heels. She couldn't tear her gaze from his hard, tight butt.

He opened a door, then her heart leaped as she real-ized there were stairs leading down.

So, have you seen his dungeon yet? Ileana had said casu-ally. *It's in the basement . . .*

She hesitated as he started down the stairs, but she forced herself to follow him. He led her to a solid oak door, then opened it.

. . . and well soundproofed. No one would hear you scream.

Her eyes widened and memories of that other dun-geon catapulted through her mind, when she'd screamed long and loud and no one had come to help.

She couldn't force herself to step inside. She noticed chains on the wall and a big *X* made of wood with chains attached to each end. A person chained to it would be forced into a spread-eagled position. Open and vulnerable.

There was a padded bench about waist high, which she could imagine being bent over to be spanked or penetrated. There were other pieces of equipment around the room, but it all faded away as she became overwhelmed with emotion. Memories of being chained and then being whipped again and again in Ileana's dungeon kept her frozen to the spot, her breath shallow and her head spinning.

"I said follow me."

At Matt's quiet but authoritative tone, Kate stepped into the dungeon without a thought, the submissive in her taking control. She crossed to where he stood by the tall bench she'd noticed earlier. He guided her to stand in front of it and pressed her forward. The top was padded leather. She heard a clinking as Matt fastened a chain to the loops on her ankle bands. He then moved in front of her and fastened her wrists to chains on the other side, holding her in the bent position.

A second later, he was behind her, stroking her bare behind, then his hard, hot body pressed close to her as he reached over the bench to cup her breasts. He stroked her nipples, then teased and pinched until her breathing became erratic, pleasure tingling through her. He glided his hands along her sides as he stood, then stroked her behind. Round and round. One hand on each cheek.

Would he pull back and smack her ass again? When the flat of his hand connected with her flesh, the sharp sound would fill the room.

She longed to hear it. To feel it.

But instead he slid his finger under the crotch of her thong and stroked her slit. She sucked in a breath as his fingers slid inside her. At the same time, he pressed his other palm to the base of the butt plug and moved it in a circle, causing the plug to swirl inside her tight channel.

He chuckled. "Clearly, you like that."

She realized she was arching back against his hand. He pushed his fingers deeper and stroked her inner passage. He tore away the thong—she hadn't realized it had Velcro on the waistband—then she felt something thicker than a finger stroke along her ass. His hot, rock-hard cock glided between her legs, over her slick slit. Back and forth. Stroking her.

He leaned close to her ear and murmured, "Do you want me to fuck you now?" His breath sent tendrils of hair fluttering along her neck. "To drive my hard cock into you right alongside this?" He wiggled the butt plug, sending electric shimmers through her.

"Oh, yes, Sir."

He positioned his cock against her opening, teasing her with the mushroom-shaped head.

"When I fill you, it will be like you have two cocks inside you. Like two men are fucking you."

"Yes," she murmured, wishing he would do it right now.

He continued to stroke her and she oozed with need. Dripping in readiness.

"Please, Mr. Pearce. I need you inside me."

His laugh rumbled from his chest. "Like this?" He drove forward and she gasped as his thick shaft filled her completely.

Without even giving her time to breathe, he thrust again. His fingers found her clit and he stroked it, and kept on while he drew back and drove forward again. Then again. Pleasure rose in her, building and building with each deep thrust. She squeezed her intimate muscles around him, making her intensely aware of the butt plug filling her other canal.

He flicked her clit while driving deep and she moaned. Blazing hot pleasure erupted inside her and she wailed. As he kept pounding into her—his hard body bouncing against her, then away with each one—the pleasure intensified, until she exploded in total bliss, her wails turning to screams.

He groaned. "Fuck, I'm coming." He jerked against her, then heat blasted her insides as he came inside her.

They both collapsed against the bench, gasping for air. She had never been so loud in her life. Being in a place where she knew no one could hear her had been liberating.

Matt's lips played along the back of her neck, sending quivers of awareness through her. "You're such a wild thing, I might have to start keeping you on a leash."

He stepped back and she felt him draw the butt plug from her opening. His hand glided down her legs, then she felt her ankles being unchained.

On a leash. For some reason, the idea excited her. She could imagine a collar around her neck with a chain attached. Maybe while she sat by his feet in front of the fireplace, him reading a paper as he stroked her hair.

He unfastened her wrists and helped her straighten up. Then he scooped her over his shoulder and stroked her bare ass as he carried her up the stairs.

Matt set Kate down at the top of the stairs, tempted to drag her off to bed and have his way with her again, but knowing they could both use a breather first. His gaze trailed over her body as she preceded him down the hall. Her thong was still in the dungeon somewhere and all she wore were a few straps of leather that covered absolutely nothing.

Her hips swayed as she walked and he longed to stroke the round, firm flesh.

Damn, his cock was rising again. It was so difficult to control his desires where Kate was involved. He would love to keep her chained to his bed and make love to her nonstop.

But life wasn't like that. And even though she was here for submissive training—and she'd made it clear to him that she wanted that to include sex—they both needed to eat occasionally.

Once they reached the living room, she turned and stood silently, waiting. Like a good sub.

"Kitchen," he said, then followed her.

She pushed open the swinging door into the kitchen and he followed her through. As soon as they were in the room, cool ceramic tile under his feet, surrounded by dark wood cupboards and the soft light of the setting sun gleaming on the black granite countertops, the desire to take her again consumed him.

He grabbed her elbow and turned her around, then his lips captured hers hungrily. She was so soft, and her lips so sweet. He dipped his tongue inside and swirled, circling his arm around her waist and drawing her tight to his body.

Oh, God, he wanted her.

He turned her and leaned her over until her breasts were crushed against the glossy granite. His cock twitched at the thought of her nipples tightening as they pressed against the cold stone. He stepped behind her and wrapped his hand around his hard cock and glided inside her. Slow and deep.

Damn it, he had to get some control. He had only this week with her; after that, their relationship would be business only. How would he cope with that? He would have to control his desire around her. He drew back and glided deep again, the intense craving for her vibrating through every part of him.

He *had* to learn control around her. And now was a good time.

He drew back and eased in again. One more time. That's all he would allow himself.

Her murmur of pleasure as he filled her deeply was almost his undoing, but with an iron will, he drew back again and this time slid out of her soft, warm body. Her sound of disappointment stroked his ego, but he stepped away.

"That's enough distraction for now." He drew her to a standing position and patted her behind. "You go upstairs and change while I make dinner. You can go to the black armoire in my room and pick something comfortable to wear for dinner." He'd bought a sexy wardrobe of clothing for her so he could dress her how he pleased as part of her submissive training. As he watched her walk away, her hips swaying, he wondered how he'd cook dinner with his cock hard and aching.

Kate was so turned on, she could barely stand it. She walked up the stairs and down the hall. Matt had more than satisfied her in the dungeon, but then when he'd glided his big, hard cock into her in the kitchen, she'd been ready for another trip to heaven. Then he'd pulled out, leaving her craving more.

Part of the training, she assumed. Keeping his sub in line.

She entered his room, and the sight of his big bed with the masculine black and gray linens tempted her. Maybe she'd lie down on that bed and stroke herself to orgasm. Would Matt be downstairs, doing the same thing? He'd been hard as a rock when he'd pulled away.

She sat down on the side of the bed, with thoughts of him stroking his hard erection. She glanced toward the dresser where he'd retrieved the butt plug earlier, wondering if he had other interesting devices in there. She stood and walked to the dresser and reached for the handle to pull open the side drawer.

But she didn't feel right going through his private stuff. At the thought, her gaze darted to the bedside table. Ileana had told her the engagement ring was still in there and Kate had almost gone searching for it. She drew in a breath and walked to the black armoire—the one Matt had told her to look inside for clothing—and opened the doors. Barely paying attention to what she was doing, she grabbed a pair of black jeans and a red pullover. She shed the leather harness and began to dress, her gaze flicking to the bedside table.

Damn Ileana for coming here and disrupting this time she had with Matt. Sowing seeds of doubt. Making her face the fact he'd lied to her.

But she knew he had probably lied about how serious his relationship with Ileana had been because he didn't want to hurt her. He had hesitated even telling her he'd dated Ileana, but he had owned up to it. The bottom line was that it didn't really matter. Kate and Matt weren't in a romantic relationship—and he resisted her attempts to change that—so he had no obligation to tell her anything about his private life.

Her gaze settled on the drawer. Had he kept the ring? Was he still pining over the woman?

She walked toward the bedside table as if drawn by a gigantic magnet. She licked her lips, hesitating. Wanting to know, but . . . not wanting to know.

She sucked in a deep breath, then grabbed the handle of the drawer and pulled it open, like ripping off a bandage. Inside was a brown leather journal, a pen, a small flashlight, and other sundry things. She glanced farther back in the drawer, and her breath caught. A black velvet box.

She picked it up with shaking fingers and snapped it open.

The soft light of the setting sun glittered on the large, solitaire diamond. It was beautiful. Simple. Elegant. Exactly what Kate would have wanted.

Her heart sank. She pushed herself up on the bed and sat cross-legged, staring at the gem. She ran her fingertip over the hard, smooth surface. She had begun to hope she might win Matt's heart again, even though he said it was impossible. She feared her own submissive nature, but even more, she feared a future without Matt in her life. She was in love with him. She realized she always had been.

If only this ring had been for her. Kate's heart ached and tears welled in her eyes.

Matt's cock still ached as he pulled the beef bourguignonne dinner from the fridge and put it into the oven to warm. He'd had it sent over from his favorite chef, along with a few other dishes, so he could spend time with Kate rather than cooking.

She was starting to trust him more, and it filled him with a deep satisfaction. She'd even let him take her to the dungeon and chain her to the punishment bench. He knew this time was helping her heal and he was glad for that.

He wondered how deep that trust had become. If he revealed what he'd done, would she be willing to forgive him? Would she believe he would never hurt her again, and allow them to move forward?

He set the timer on the oven, then headed for the stairs. Kate was probably in her room, waiting for his next command. He'd get dressed, then invite her down-stairs for a drink by the fire before dinner. He padded down the hall, his bare feet making no sound on the hardwood floors. As he stepped toward the doorway, he noticed Kate sitting cross-legged on his bed, now dressed in jeans and a sweater.

He smiled, rather wishing she still wore the harness, so he could enjoy the view of her sumptuous body. His cock stirred at the memory of her in the crouched posi-tion she'd adopted earlier when he'd come home from the office, her naked folds open to him.

Her gaze jerked toward him and his heart wrenched at the sight of tears glittering in her eyes.

"Oh, Matt, I didn't hear you."

Her voice sounded anxious. Almost panicky. It was then he noticed she held something in her hand. Despite her quick movement to try and hide it, the sparkle of the diamond had been unmistakable before she'd closed the box and tucked it beside her knee.

She'd found the ring. His gut clenched.

"What are you doing with that, Kate?" He grabbed his robe from the back of the chair and pulled it on.

Her cheeks were flushed as she stared at him, guilt suffusing her eyes. "I'm sorry, Matt. I shouldn't have gone through your drawer, but . . . when Ileana told me—"

"Ileana? What the fuck were you doing talking to Ileana?"

Her gaze dropped. "She came by when you were gone this afternoon. I answered the door and she just pushed her way in."

"And you two just started chatting calmly and she told you about the ring?"

He walked toward her and held out his hand. There was no point ignoring what it was. Kate hesitated, then placed the velvet ring box in his hand. He walked to the bedside table and placed it in the drawer, near the back, then closed it.

Whatever Ileana had told Kate, it wasn't going to be good. He did not want Kate to know the story behind the ring, but Ileana's plans rarely matched his. He just couldn't figure out what Ileana would have to gain by telling Kate about it.

Kate hadn't answered his question yet. "So, what did she say?"

Kate shifted under Matt's intense scrutiny. She pushed herself from the bed and walked toward the window, gathering her wits. Drawing in a breath, she pushed aside the guilt of being caught with the evidence that she'd invaded his private space, drew back her shoulders, and turned to face him.

"You told me that you only dated Ileana for a short time and that it meant nothing."

His expression didn't change. "That's right."

She'd expected some hint of guilt.

"But . . . that's a lie."

"Kate, what did she tell you?"

Kate wrapped her arms around herself and started to pace. "She knew where everything was. She knew her way around the kitchen and how to work the sound system. She knew about the dungeon." She stared up at Matt. "She knew this house."

Ileana had managed to make Kate feel like the outsider.

"We were friends before we dated," Matt said, "and even after we broke up, she was the head of my legal team. She was often over here to discuss contracts, or for social gatherings. She also helped me furnish the place."

A tremor crawled along Kate's spine. Suddenly, Ileana's presence seemed to surround her. No wonder the furniture felt a little more formal than she would have expected for Matt. Had Ileana picked out all the furniture? Had she picked out this bed? Had she chosen the linens?

How often had she and Matt made love in that bed? Had Matt spoken soft words of love in her ear?

"She said you dated a lot longer than a few months."

His eyebrows arched. "Really? How long did she say?"

"She said you were still together when you saw me in the mall a few weeks ago."

"And you believed her?"

She shrugged. "No, not exactly. I mean, I didn't know what to believe, and she didn't seem to care if I believed her or not."

"Of course. She knows that would work better. Drop a few comments. Lead you where she wants you to go." He scowled. "Just enough to sow the seeds of doubt." His lips compressed. "Kate, I thought you'd finally come to trust me again."

"I did." She sucked in a breath. "I do."

It was true. She'd even gotten past her hesitation at the dungeon door because, deep inside, she knew Matt would never purposely hurt her.

"And I understand that if you had a more serious relationship with Ileana," she said, "you might feel there was no reason to tell me. You and I aren't in a romantic relationship, so it's really none of my business, and it would make things awkward between us. You might feel it would hurt me to know about it."

"Kate, I'm not hiding anything from you. I was never in a serious relationship with Ileana."

Kate's throat clenched and she forced her gaze to meet his. "Then why did you propose to her?"

"What? That's crazy. You can't actually believe that."

Her eyebrows arched. "What about the ring?"

"The fact I have a ring doesn't prove—"

"She showed me pictures of you sliding the ring on

her finger." The look of joy in Matt's eyes in that picture still haunted her.

He paused, his brows drawn together in bewilderment. "A picture?" He frowned, then sighed. "Right. I asked her to come with me to pick out a ring because I wanted a woman's perspective. While we were shopping, she asked the salesman to take some pictures of her trying the ring on. It wasn't a picture of me proposing."

"Oh. So, there's someone else?" Her heart clenched at the thought. But of course he would have been dating other women over the past two years, so it made sense that he would become serious about one of them.

His expression closed up. "That's not important. The point is, I'm not involved with Ileana, and I definitely never proposed to her. Nor do I intend to." He locked his gaze on hers. "I didn't lie to you."

She stared at him, not sure what to think. Who was this other woman and why didn't he want to talk about her? And if he had another woman in his life, why was he spending this time with Kate? Having sex with her.

Unless the woman had turned him down.

"I believe you," she said.

"Good."

"Matt, this other woman—"

"Look, Kate, as you already pointed out, you and I are not in a romantic relationship. What goes on in my personal life has nothing to do with you."

A shiver ran through her at his cool, businesslike tone.

"I would still like to help you come to terms with your submissive side," he continued, "because I think it will help you in future relationships, but if you don't want to stay, I'll understand." He turned and walked toward the door. "I'll leave you to think about it. You can find me in my study."

Matt swirled the drink in his glass, watching the liquid absently. Damn it, he never should have brought Kate here. He'd thought it was helping her, and with respect to her healing over the past events, it probably was, but it wasn't helping either of them get past what was between them. He didn't know if she would leave now or not, but it would probably be for the best.

A tap sounded at the door. Time for the verdict.

"Come in."

He set his glass on the desk as the door opened. Kate stepped inside.

"Hi." She glanced around nervously, taking in the hunter-green walls and the dark wood furniture of his masculine den. Her gaze settled on his and she shifted a little, clearly nervous.

"So what have you decided?" he asked.

"I want to stay."

The knot in his stomach loosened. Maybe it would be better if she left, but he was glad she was staying.

But he knew he had to keep control of things.

"Fine. Then I think it's time we ramp things up."

She pushed her fingers in her jeans pockets. "Okay."

"This will only work if you trust me totally."

She gazed at him solemnly and nodded. "I do."

He didn't believe that was completely true, but they would proceed from here.

"Good. For the rest of the week, we will stay in role. You will do exactly what I say. When I say. Without question. Without thought. Is that clear?"

"Yes, Sir."

"Good. Now take off your clothes."

She blinked, but then she began stripping away her garments. Her sweater and jeans landed in a heap on the floor, then she reached behind herself and unfastened her bra. His heartbeat increased as she drew the garment away, revealing her perfect breasts. So pert and round. The nipples hardened as his gaze caressed them. She tucked her thumbs under the waistband of her panties and pushed them down, then kicked them away. Now she stood before him totally naked. His cock swelled at the erotic sight.

"Come over here and kneel in front of me."

As she walked toward the desk, he opened the drawer and retrieved the black leather collar with silver spikes he had picked out for her for this week. It was a symbol of the bond between a Dom and his sub. Of trust and obedience on her part. It hadn't been appropriate to give it to her at the beginning of the week, because she hadn't been ready. In fact, it probably wasn't appropriate to give it to her at all, because they would never be true Dom and sub. Eventually, she would bond with someone else in that way. That's why they were doing this whole thing. So she could eventually find her happiness with someone else.

Even though the two of them were not meant to be, however, by giving her this collar, he was claiming her on some level. He would always know she had submitted to him and accepted his collar.

He turned his chair as she rounded the desk and approached him. She sank to her knees in front of him.

"Lift your hair," he instructed.

She gathered her long, auburn hair in her hands and lifted it out of the way. He wrapped the collar around her neck and fastened it. She released her hair and it spilled around her shoulders in soft waves. The black collar looked good against her pale flesh, surrounded by her burnished copper hair, the silver spikes glinting in the light.

"Now, suck my cock, slave."

A shiver danced down Kate's spine. He'd never called her slave before. It made her feel so . . . controlled.

"Yes, Mr. Pearce."

He still wore his robe, so she reached for the front of the garment below the sash and parted the fabric. His already rising cock popped forward. She gazed in his eyes, as she wrapped her hand around his shaft and brought the tip to her mouth.

"And don't make me come."

She nodded as she licked him, watching his eyelids flicker as heat suffused his midnight blue eyes. She swirled her tongue over the hot flesh, dabbing at the tiny hole, tasting the salty drop of liquid oozing there. She spiraled downward, then wrapped her lips around him and swallowed the mushroom-shaped head into her mouth. He tucked his hand behind her head as she slid down his shaft, opening her throat to take him deep.

She glided up and down, his big cock filling her mouth and throat.

"Now, lick my balls."

She drew his shaft from her mouth and tucked her hand under his shaven balls, then lifted them. She licked, then nibbled them with her lips. She drew one in her mouth and bounced it on her tongue, then sucked lightly. Her other hand still grasped his erection, stroking up and down. She licked and cajoled his soft sack in her mouth, until he moaned.

His fingers forked through her hair. "Now, suck my cock again."

She released his balls and pressed his cock to her lips again, then took him inside. He was getting close so she had to be careful. He'd told her not to allow him to come.

She glided down, his rock-hard flesh filling her mouth as she took him deep. She moved slowly up and swirled her tongue around the underside of his corona.

"Yes, I like that." His hand, still wrapped around her head, drew her forward until his cock filled her throat.

She glided back and he pulled her forward again. He was getting close and she tried to draw away, but he guided her head forward and back, faster and faster. He was controlling her. Forcing her to his will. Excitement skittered through her.

He arched forward, groaning. Liquid heat filled her mouth and she swallowed as best she could, but some spilled from her lips.

He released her and she eased back, allowing his cock to fall from her lips.

His stern gaze locked onto her. "You disobeyed me. You were not to make me come."

"Yes, Sir. I'm sorry."

"Stand up."

She stood and he turned his chair, guiding her in front of him, facing the desk.

"Lean over."

She leaned over the desk, her breasts resting against the hard, cool mahogany.

His fingers stroked over her ass, then he smacked. Hard. The tingling danced along her skin, then he smacked again. Then a third time. The stinging increasing with each slap. Heat rushed through her. She gasped as he smacked again.

Then his fingers stroked over her heated flesh. Lightly.

"You have a beautiful ass. Especially when it's glowing red like this."

He stroked round and round, then he parted her cheeks and leaned forward. She moaned at the feel of his tongue gliding along her slick folds, then pressing into her and wiggling inside, sending tremors through her.

His finger found her clit and he teased. Pleasure swamped her senses and she sucked in air. He teased her until she felt the pleasure swell, closing in on an orgasm. Her breathing accelerated as he stroked and licked her. The pleasure swelled and she could feel it . . . so close.

Then he stopped.

He stood up behind her and hooked his finger through a loop on the collar, then pulled her to a standing position. A moment later, she was following him out the door. The collar tugged on her neck as he led her down the hall. He opened the door to the basement.

"You know where I want you to go."

"To the dungeon, Sir."

"That's right."

He released the ring on her collar and followed her down the stairs, then opened the door to the dungeon and gestured for her to precede him in. Once inside, he hooked his finger through the collar ring again and led her across the room, passing the punishment bench where he'd made love to her earlier. He stopped at a wide table, with padding on top.

"Climb on top and assume the position."

She climbed onto the table and knelt, then leaned over just as she had on his bed when he'd returned from the office. This was the position he'd first shown her in her apartment when she'd asked about the training—when she'd insisted he show her one of the more daring positions—and now it seemed to be his favorite. As she pushed her ass in the air, knowing he was staring at her damp folds from behind, she realized she felt the same way. She felt vulnerable and open to him. He could do anything to her. And that excited her.

"I want you to spread yourself open and show me your most intimate parts. Then I want you to touch yourself."

She reached behind herself, grasped her ass cheeks, then separated them. He'd be able to see her glistening opening easily. Then she raised her belly and slid one hand underneath and up to stroke her slippery slit.

"I like that," he murmured. "Now, find your clit and stroke it."

She glided through her folds and found the hot little button, then flicked over it. Pleasure swelled through her, but she slowed down, knowing he wouldn't let her come yet.

"Yes, that's lovely. Are you turned on?"

"Yes, Mr. Pearce."

"Could you come right now?"

"Yes, Sir."

"Good. Now stop."

He walked to a wooden cupboard along the wall and pulled open a door, revealing several floggers. He selected one that was pink and seemed to be suede. He opened a drawer and picked up something small, too—she couldn't see what it was—and slipped it into the pocket of his robe. She stiffened a bit as he returned to her carrying the flogger, its half-inch strips of suede attached to a matching suede-wrapped handle. He held it in front of her, so she could see it up close, then he dragged it over her back. The suede was soft against her skin. The gentle way he stroked her back with it, and maybe the fact it was pink, relaxed her.

"I'm going to punish you in a few minutes, but first I'm going to get you ready."

His hand slipped into his robe pocket as he walked around behind her. He stroked her ass, then glided his fingers along her slit. She felt something cold and hard press against her, then he slipped something inside her wet opening. She squeezed around it, gripping it inside her.

"Now, you need to help me get ready."

She glanced up and realized he was in front of her again. He slipped off his robe and pressed his cockhead to her mouth. She took him inside and sucked. Suddenly, the thing inside her began to vibrate. Her gaze darted to his and he showed her a small remote control in his hand. The vibration stopped and she sucked on him again. His cock grew harder and the device started to vibrate again. Then it stopped. He pulled his cock from her mouth and grabbed his robe from the ground. He held a small bottle of lube, which he spread over his cock, then walked behind her.

He pressed his slick cockhead between her cheeks and teased her by gliding along her ass. Then he positioned himself against her back opening and pressed forward. She relaxed, then pushed her muscles until his cockhead slipped inside her. He kept pushing forward, easing his cock deeper. The little device in her vagina began vibrating again and she moaned. His cock was so big inside her ass, and the tremors in her front passage delighted her.

"I'm going to punish you now."

"Yes, Sir."

With the feel of his big cock filling her, and the little device whirring inside her, she was distracted from her nervousness. He dragged the flogger sideways across her body. His cock slid back along her canal, then forward again. The vibrations slowed as he whisked the flogger from side to side across her skin, lightly, caressing her with a gentle rhythm of delightful sensations.

She couldn't believe how wonderful the flogger felt. The wide strips gliding across her back felt more like a massage than a whipping. But, of course, she knew she could trust Matt to make punishment a pleasure for her. She was sure this flogger, if used differently, could cause pain. But Matt wouldn't do that to her.

"Will you obey me next time?"

"Yes, Sir. I'm sorry."

The suede swirled over her back and the device whirred faster inside her. She clamped tight around it, squeezing it inside her as Matt's big cock glided faster into her.

"Good. Your apology pleases me."

She groaned as he plunged deep, then the flogging stopped and he slid his hand around her waist and drew her up, until he pressed her tight against his torso. He stroked her breasts with the soft suede of the flogger as he continued to bang into her. Pleasure rippled through her. From the vibrator humming inside her. The soft suede brushing her nipples. His big cock driving into her.

"Oh, God, yes." Blissful sensations fluttered through her and she arched against him. Then she gasped as an orgasm exploded inside her.

He continued to ride her, his cock pumping deep into her, driving her pleasure higher. Then he groaned his release and held her tight to his body.

Matt erupted inside her, groaning at the potent pleasure. Damn, it was so intense with Kate. Her body pressed tight to his, her back passage gripping him like a vise. He drew out and knew he had to have her again. He grabbed a moist towelette from the small drawer in the table and wiped off, then he grabbed her hips and flipped her over.

He slipped his fingers into her slit and pulled the still-vibrating device from her wet depths, then he pushed his still-hard cock inside her. She sat up and into his arms, her legs wrapping around his waist. He kissed her, his tongue delving deep, dancing with her own. She drove her tongue back into his mouth, her lips moving on his with passion.

He thrust his hips forward and she groaned. He pumped inside her, loving the feel of her velvet sheath around him. She clung to him, her face a vision of rapture. She sucked in a breath, then moaned again. Her eyes fell closed and he pressed his lips to her neck as he continued to drive into her. Giving her pleasure.

She wailed in ecstasy and he kept going. He wasn't going to come again so soon, so he just enjoyed giving her this pleasure.

Finally, she slumped against him, her head lolling on his shoulder. He picked her up, still embedded inside her, and carried her up the two flights of stairs to his room.

Kate woke up, snuggled against Matt, his arms still around her. She felt so warm and protected in his arms. He had even used a flogger on her last night, and she had loved it. There'd been no residual fear from that other incident. No fear at all, since she knew Matt would never hurt her.

Of course, he must have chosen a pink flogger for a reason. It made her think of soft, cute things, not pain. And he had so lovingly stroked across her back with it.

She could imagine using it on Matt. Brushing it across his broad, naked chest. Then maybe flicking it, just to get his attention—and make him a little nervous—then stroking again.

But when did the sub get to punish the Dom?

She'd have to think about that. Maybe she could pretend to capture him. Chain him up and have her way with him.

She was getting hot just thinking about it. But there were no chains handy. She grinned. Of course, maybe she could bind him with her powers of sexual persuasion.

Matt awoke to Kate's soft hands on his already swelling cock. He groaned at the sweet warmth of her mouth surrounding him and her throat enveloping him. She took him deep several times, then prowled over him. As she sat on his pelvis—her warm, wet folds pressed against the ridge of his cock—she grasped his wrists and pressed them beside his head and winked.

"I've chained you down, *Sir.*" She said the honorific with sass, her eyes gleaming. "Now you're under my control."

He shouldn't allow her to do this. He was training her to be a sub, in order for her to accept that side of herself.

But he couldn't resist her playful sexiness . . . and the heat of her slick body gliding up and down his cock as she pivoted her hips on him.

She reached down and grasped his cock, then slid it inside her.

"Oh, yeah."

She leaned forward and brushed her breast against his mouth. He opened and licked her tight nipple, then pulled it inside and sucked. She moaned and pressed forward more. He sucked until she tugged her breast free, then pressed the other forward. He licked the newly offered nipple, then pinched it lightly with his teeth. She gasped, then pushed it forward until he sucked deeply.

She sat up, cupping her breasts and stroking the nipples as she moved up and down on him. He watched her fingers toy with the hard nubs, his cock swelling even more inside her hot depths. She squeezed him and he groaned, then she stroked her hands over his chest and pinched his nipples as she increased the rhythm, her body gliding on him faster. Taking him deeper.

He watched her face, glowing in pleasure, her eyes gleaming brightly. The cadence of her breathing told him she was close. And so was he.

If his hands weren't bound by imaginary chains, he'd reach up and stroke her sweet breasts, but he satisfied himself with watching them bounce gently with her movement.

She tightened around him, then threw her head back and moaned. The sight of her in full orgasm sent him shooting over the edge and he erupted inside her.

"Oh, God, Kate. You are so sexy."

She smiled and snuggled up against him, his cock still buried in her depths. "And so are you."

She nuzzled his neck, then lifted her head and kissed him. Their gazes locked and her smile faded as she stared deeply into his eyes.

"I love you, Matt."

As soon as she'd said it, Kate's stomach dropped. What had she been thinking?

But for one brief second, she saw the same feelings gleaming in his dark eyes. And then they blanked out. He was so good at hiding his feelings, but she'd seen them. He loved her.

He gazed at her, and stroked his hand through her hair—so much for the imaginary chains—then he drew her to his body again, cupping her head to his chest. She could hear his heart beating. She was warm tucked against him like this, his big cock still inside her. She closed her eyes and let the steady rhythm lull her, until she finally fell asleep.

When she awoke again, he was still inside her, but he was growing hard again. She glanced at the bedside clock and realized she'd only been asleep about twenty minutes, but tendrils of sunshine were streaming in the window.

She arched against him, enjoying the feel of his rapidly hardening cock inside her, but he flattened his hand on her lower back, stilling her movements.

"I think it's time for more sleep, not sex."

She smiled. "I'm not tired."

"That's because you've been sleeping. I couldn't do that with your soft, sexy body as a blanket."

She laughed, then leaned in and kissed his neck. "Poor man. I feel so sorry for you." At that, she spiraled her hips, loving the feel of his big cock swirling inside her.

He tipped onto his side and drew away from her, his big cock pulling out of her.

"I would think you'd love to wake up to a willing woman wanting to have hot morning sex."

But when she gazed at his face, he wore a serious expression.

"That little episode was fun, but we're here to train you as a sub so we need to stay focused."

She stroked his cheek. "Matt, I think you've done a great job helping me accept my submissive side. I'm loving being your sub." She nuzzled his neck.

"That's good. Then"—he hesitated for a moment and she glanced up at him—"maybe we're done."

"What do you mean 'done'?"

He sat up, his body sliding away from her as he did. She sat cross-legged facing him.

"You said it yourself. You love being a sub. It sounds like we can end the training period."

"I said I love being *your* sub," she corrected. "I'm getting the idea that when you say you want to end the training period, that means you want to end our week together, too."

"That's right."

She frowned. "This isn't about the training. This is about the fact I said I love you."

Damn it. Matt had hoped to avoid this. He had hoped she'd take the hint and let it drop.

"Kate, I already told you, there is no future for us."

"I don't believe you. I saw it in your eyes. I see it now. You love me, too."

"Kate, don't . . ." He turned his gaze away from her.

She grasped his chin with her soft fingers and turned him back to face her.

"Look, Matt. I know that you were hurt by some other woman. The woman you bought the ring for. And I assumed that meant you didn't love me, even though you are going to such lengths to help me. But last night . . . when I said the words . . . I could see the same thing in your eyes."

She stroked his cheek, and her soft touch—paired with the love in her eyes—sent warmth shimmering through him.

"Look, Matt. I love you and I'm not giving up on you. So, either tell me you don't love me, or tell me why we can't be together."

His gut clenched. He wished he could just lie. Tell her he didn't love her. But the alternative was to tell her what a bastard he'd been two years ago.

"Kate, we can't be together. Can't you just accept that?"

She shook her head, her intense blue gaze locked on him.

He sighed and pushed his feet off the side of the bed, then sat up.

"All right. I should have told you before, but then you wouldn't have let me help you. And I needed to do that. I needed to try and set things right."

"What are you talking about, Matt?"

He stared into her eyes, soaking in the love shining there, knowing the words he was about to say would extinguish that love completely.

"The reason we can't be together is because of what I did two years ago. After you left me."

The Surrender

Kate's heart thundered in her chest. They couldn't be together because of something Matt did?

"Wait, I don't understand. What about the other woman?"

"You mean Ileana? I told you, we only dated for a few months."

She didn't mean Ileana, but a growing dread prevented her from changing the line of conversation.

Matt's gaze fell on her face and he paused. "Kate, I know Ileana caused you a great deal of pain, and it must be hard to know that she and I were together, but you've got to remember that I had no idea what happened. What she did to you."

Kate hugged her knees and nodded. "I know. But it's hard knowing you were with her." She glanced around the room. "Knowing she was here with you. That you shared this bed."

The woman had caused them so much grief.

Matt put his arms around her and drew her close to his solid body. She rested her head against his chest, taking solace in the fact she was here with him now, and that Ileana was out of the picture.

"How long exactly did you date her?"

"It started a few weeks after the party. It became clear that you weren't going to answer my calls or e-mails. That you had decided to end it with me totally."

At the pain in his voice, Kate took his hand and squeezed it. His warm fingers wrapped around hers.

"I was devastated and Ileana was there for me, listening, helping. I know now that must have been her plan all along. To drive you away, then insinuate herself into my life."

"Why would she do that?" Kate gazed into his midnight blue eyes and was surprised to see his lips turn up in a smile.

"Well, I *am* considered quite a catch, you know."

She returned his smile and stroked his cheek, loving the feel of stubble against her fingertips.

"I know you are." She pressed her lips to his neck

and kissed the whisker-roughened skin. "So why did you stop seeing her?"

He shrugged. "I was grief-stricken but I wasn't blind. It didn't take long to realize she was manipulative and ruthlessly ambitious. Within the space of a few months, she'd advanced from being a lawyer helping me out with a charity project, to being the prime contact between her law firm and my corporation—which was their biggest client—to being my girlfriend. It quickly became apparent to me that I was a means to an end."

"So you broke it off with her?"

He nodded. "She didn't love me. And I didn't love her. I woke up one morning and realized there was nothing between us. That she was just a rebound relationship. Of course, I'd known it all along, but wouldn't listen to the voice shouting inside me." His lips brushed her forehead in a light kiss. "We fool ourselves at times like that. When we're hurting. I wanted to be needed. To be loved."

Kate's heart ached at his totally sincere words, knowing she'd been the cause of his pain. While at the same time, she'd been in pain herself.

Damn Ileana.

"But I finally figured it out, and I broke it off with her."

"What did she do?" Kate couldn't imagine that Ileana would have taken it well.

"Surprisingly, she took it in stride. I think what she really cared about was securing a senior position in her firm. If she could have married me and been a wealthy man's wife, that would have been a bonus, but I suspect she wouldn't have liked the limitations that situation would impose on her. She didn't love me and I think she already had her eye on another man. A partner at her firm."

"But when you broke up with her, she stayed as the contact person for your company?"

"Sure. Just because she and I didn't work out didn't mean I would jeopardize her job. I could work with her in a professional capacity and I didn't have to deal with her very often anyway. Mostly she dealt with my senior staff." He tucked his finger under her chin and lifted it, their gazes aligning. "Remember, I had no idea how vicious she'd been with regards to you. After you told me what really happened, and Ileana's part in it, I went back and had her removed as our contact immediately. I told the senior partner of her firm that I didn't want her having anything to do with my business."

She nodded, and he glided his finger along her cheek, then she settled her head against his chest again.

"As it turns out, he was only too happy to replace her. It seems she'd been indiscreet while having an affair with two of the partners at the same time, causing jealousy and a lot of friction around the office. The only

reason they'd kept her around was because of her connection to me. As soon as I severed that, they fired her."

"So she's out of a job?"

"Kate, you can't tell me you feel sorry for her."

"No, it's not that. When she was here, she wanted to
get the ring, saying it was hers and she shouldn't have
given it back to you."

"It was never hers."

Kate nodded. "But do you think she would actually
have taken the ring? She said something about moving
to California to start again, and that the ring would go a
long way toward a down payment on a house."

"She would certainly have trouble finding work
in New York again after the problems she's caused. I
wouldn't put it past her to take the ring. Then, if I tried
to charge her with theft, she might find a way to turn it
around on you if you had let her take the ring, or just
deny that she had it." He shrugged. "Or she probably
just expected that I couldn't be bothered going after her
for it."

She tightened her arms around him. "I'm just glad
she's no longer a part of our life."

Our life. She gazed up at Matt. She so much wanted
a shared life with him. She loved him so much her heart
ached.

But there was something standing in the way of that,
and she had to know what it was.

"Matt, last night you wouldn't talk about it, but I really want to know about the woman you bought the ring for."

"Kate . . ."

"No, please. I know she hurt you. And I assume you still love her. But you need to move on with your life. You need to get over her."

"Kate, that's what I've been trying to do." He placed his hands on her shoulders and pressed her back. Their bodies parted and the comfort of being close to him slipped away. He stared at her, pain emanating from his eyes. "But it's harder than you know."

"Why, Matt? Who is she? What did she do to you?"

"She didn't do anything. It's what I did."

She looked at him, confused. She couldn't imagine Matt doing anything that would drive a woman away.

He tucked his finger under her chin and tilted her face toward him. "And the woman is you."

She shook her head. "I don't understand."

"Kate, I bought the ring for you. Before the party. Ileana came with me to pick it out. I was going to propose the following weekend."

Her chin trembled as she gazed at him. "You were going to propose . . . to me?"

He nodded. "I had it all planned out. I booked a romantic getaway and I was going to propose on bended knee under the stars. I bought this house for us to live in." He stroked her cheek with yearning in his eyes.

"Oh, Matt." She surged forward and kissed him, her lips moving on his passionately.

His arms swept around her as he answered her loving kiss.

"Oh, Matt, I love you."

His eyes turned guarded and he tried to draw back, but she tightened her arms around him.

"Kate, I shouldn't have told you that. It was selfish and—"

She stopped his words with another kiss, wanting to break down his resolve.

"No, I won't let you take it back. You love me. No matter what else you have to say, no matter what happens in the future, right now I know you love me." She stroked his cheek, tenderness flooding through her. "And I love you. Give me this."

Emotions warred in his eyes, then he relented and dragged her against his solid chest again. His mouth consumed hers, his tongue delving deep. She opened, welcoming him. Her heart pounded in her chest as their tongues danced. She ran her hands along his cheek, stroking his stubbly chin, elation flooding through her.

"No, Kate. There's more. I need to tell you—"

She covered his mouth again, at the same time grasping his shoulders and pushing him back on the bed.

She locked gazes with him. "No, you don't." She ran her hands along his shoulders, then down his muscular chest. "Not now."

Because she knew she didn't want to hear it.

"Right now, I want this." She leaned forward and nipped his shoulder, then kissed her way down his chest. "Knowing you love me. Sharing that love." She dragged her tongue over his tight nipple. "I won't allow anything to ruin it." She licked his other nipple, then sucked, eliciting a groan.

"Kate." He rolled her over until his solid masculine body hovered over her.

For a moment, she thought he was going to release her and roll away, but then his lips swooped down and claimed hers again. When he released her mouth, she was breathless.

"I do love you, Kate." His dark gaze pierced her. "And I want this just as much as you do."

The passion of his kiss unnerved her, but she opened to him, then glided her tongue inside his mouth, exploring the hot depths. Their tongues tangled until finally she drew back and sucked in air.

"I love you, Matt." She pressed on his chest and he allowed her to roll him onto his back, then she prowled over him, resting her knees on either side of his thighs, his swelling shaft a hard ridge against her aching wet flesh.

She stroked his chest with both hands, loving the feel of solid muscle under her fingertips. He ran his hands over her shoulders, then down her chest, his fingertips sending electrical impulses of pleasure rippling through her. When his thumb brushed her nipple, she gasped and arched toward him. He drew her forward and licked her nipple, then suckled lightly. Her head spun as she moaned at the exquisite sensation.

She glided her body forward, then back, dragging her slick opening over his growing shaft. It was so hard and solid. Stroking her. He drew her down until her breasts crushed against his hard chest and he cupped her cheek, then their lips met again. She glided her tongue inside him, reveling in the warmth of him, and the magic of sharing this closeness.

"Matt, make love to me."

He smiled, lighting up his whole face. "I will, my sweet." He stroked her cheek, then rolled her over until she lay trapped beneath his solid body. "But after I taste you."

He prowled downward with a beaming smile, then pressed her legs wide. His mouth lightly brushed her upper thigh and she arched. When his tongue grazed her slick folds, then pressed into them, she moaned.

"Oh, Matt. Yes."

He licked inside her as his fingers explored. Two slid inside, just a little, and his tongue found her clit. A thin, trailing moan erupted from her as he licked and cajoled. His fingers glided deeper and she arched. Her fingers twined through his hair as her nerve endings blasted her with pure sensation. She drifted on a cloud of bliss.

Matt loved her.

He suckled her bud and she gasped again, then exploded into ecstasy, her fingers tightening around his scalp. He continued sucking and licking as pleasure blasted through her.

Finally, she collapsed, and he gazed up at her, his eyes gleaming.

A deep need pulsed within her. She needed to join with him. To feel his hot, hard shaft inside her. Her need must have shone brightly in her eyes, because he kissed up her body, then settled his knees between her thighs.

"I want you, Kate."

She nodded. "Yes." She stroked his shoulders. "Fill me, Matt. I want you inside me."

His lips found hers in a potently gentle kiss, as his rock-hard flesh brushed her opening. Slowly, his solid erection pushed into her, her soft flesh stretching around him as she accepted him into her body.

"Oh, Matt." She gazed into his midnight eyes and could barely believe the depth of the love shining there. It blazed like the noonday sun, filling her with warmth.

He surged forward, until he was fully immersed. She clung to him, holding him tight against her, wishing she could keep him this close forever. He twitched inside her and she laughed in pure joy. He nuzzled her neck.

"My God, you are so soft." He kissed her, his tongue gliding deep.

She stroked it with her own, reveling in the powerful intimacy of the moment. Then their gazes locked and it was as if the world around them melted away. Only the two of them existed in this place, in this time. In a brief moment of eternity.

Kate knew she would never stop loving this man. No matter what happened. No matter what he told her.

"Kate, what is it?"

She realized a tear had welled in her eye and she shook her head. "Nothing, I just love you so much."

A shadow flickered in his eyes, but he melded his lips with hers and the intensity of his kiss took her breath away.

"And I love you."

Then he drew back and surged forward again. His hot, hard shaft filled her and she tightened around him, trying to keep him inside her, but he glided away, then surged deep again.

"Oh, Matt." Her reedy words ended on a whimper as his hard, masculine body crushed her to the bed.

He moved back and forth within her, his powerful thrusts driving her to heaven. She whimpered again, clinging to his shoulders.

"Kate, come for me, sweetheart. I want to see your face in the sweet state of bliss."

The pleasure already swelled within her, but his words sent her spinning over the edge.

"Oh, yes. Oh, Matt." She wailed as blissful streaks of pure ecstasy glided through her. She arched against him.

He thrust again and she wailed as an orgasm exploded within her, with Matt deep inside her, his arms wrapped around her, the two of them joined as one.

She squeezed his hard flesh inside her.

"Kate. Yes." He groaned and hot liquid filled her, driving her pleasure higher.

They rode the wave of ecstasy together, clinging to each other. Finally, they collapsed together, gasping for air.

Matt rolled back, taking Kate with him, holding her tight to his chest. She snuggled against him and he stroked her long hair as their rapid breathing slowed to a more normal rate. Her breath brushed across his skin, stirring the hair on his chest.

God, he wanted to hold her like this forever. To make her his wife and keep her close to him.

If only he could undo the past and make everything okay. If only he could just hide away what he'd done and move forward from here.

But she knew he had something to tell her. There was no way to escape from what he'd done any longer.

Kate tightened her arms around his waist. "Matt, I can feel you slipping away from me."

He kissed the top of her head. "No, sweetheart. Never."

She drew in a breath and pushed herself to a sitting position. "I'd like to believe that, but you said there's something you need to tell me. That there's a reason we can't be together. As much as I don't want to hear it, I need to know what it is so we can get past it."

He sat up beside her and gazed into her sincere blue eyes. Hope welled in him that maybe, just maybe, she would understand and they could get past it, then forge a loving relationship together.

He took her hand and kissed it, then held it within both of his.

"Kate, when you walked out on me two years ago, I was devastated. I knew you'd been holding back, that there was something about our relationship that bothered you . . ." He squeezed her hand. "Actually, I knew it had to do with your submissiveness . . . but I really thought we'd work it out. I bought the ring . . . I planned on proposing the following weekend. I thought once you knew how serious I was about you, that we could talk about it. That we could work everything out."

He released her hand and stood up. He couldn't be this close to her when he told her. He needed distance. He needed to feel that old pain . . . so he could explain properly.

"When we went to Ileana's party, I couldn't believe that you'd just ditch me like that. That you'd go off with another man."

"Why did you believe it, Matt?"

He gazed at her, shaking his head. How could she not understand?

"Kate, you kept a part of yourself separate from me. Closed off. You never let me inside. That means that every day I felt rejected by you. Every day I felt the 'keep out' sign you had posted on your heart. I loved you. I thought you loved me. So a part of me couldn't believe you would just walk away. But another part . . . the part that felt that rejection so deeply . . . expected it."

Kate stared at him with wide eyes, her head shaking.

"But, Matt, I never wanted to hurt you. I never would have just walked away."

"But you had thought about leaving, right?"

Her lips pursed and he could see the truth written across her face.

Her hands clenched around the sheets. "I told you how much my submissiveness disturbed me. It wasn't you. It was how I acted."

"It doesn't matter how much you say it wasn't me, it *was* me you were rejecting."

"Only because you were the one who brought out that side of me."

"Do you think that made the rejection any easier?"

Her big blue eyes gleamed as she gazed at him. "Oh, Matt, but I didn't leave you. I probably wouldn't have."

His hands balled into fists. "But in a way you did, every time you held a part of yourself back. And then you did for real." He waved away her protest. "I know now that you left because of the lies you'd been told about me, but from my point of view at the time, you left me. Because you didn't really love me. It was a rejection so complete, and so sudden, it tore my heart in two."

He stared at her, the pain of that rejection searing through him. Her gaze darted away from him.

"Don't get me wrong, Kate. I know it wasn't your fault. Now. But back then, I thought you'd simply found someone else and walked out of my life. I didn't understand how you could do it in such a callous way and, at first, I didn't believe it. That's why I kept calling you. But you wouldn't answer me. Then you asked to be taken off the project for my company. I couldn't argue with the facts." He turned his palms to her imploringly. "What else was I supposed to believe?"

She stood up. "Matt, I'm sorry for what you went through." She stepped toward him, but he shook his head and turned away.

"Don't be. I have more to tell you." He paced across the room, then turned to face her again, a comfortable distance between them.

"A few weeks after it all happened, I was at a fund-raiser and the president of the consulting firm you worked for approached me. We talked a bit about general matters, then the conversation turned to the usual business stuff. He wanted to ensure the transition to a new project leader had gone smoothly, after you'd left the project. He knew I didn't deal with the project directly, but that I keep pretty close tabs on everything that goes on in my company. After that, he mentioned that he'd asked for a recommendation from my personnel manager to help place you on another project, and he hadn't heard back. He asked if I could expedite the process because they needed the reference for a new client project. That this client was getting impatient and nothing could move forward until they had the reference. He assumed I'd give you a glowing review."

He and Kate had been careful not to let anyone on the business side know about their romance, but everyone knew that Matt thought highly of Kate and her work. She did excel at what she did and he ensured his staff knew he recognized that.

"Of course, I couldn't tell him I would give you a good reference. Even though that would be the professional thing to do, I really didn't give a shit about professionalism at that point. I was hurting."

"You gave me a negative review?"

"No, I gave you no recommendation at all. But it seems, at that same party, Ileana, who was my companion that night, made a point of giving your boss a *friendly* word of warning that you would never be welcome at Cutting Edge Industries again, or at any of my other companies."

"He wouldn't have liked that. You were our biggest client."

"That's right. I knew what Ileana had said to him, and I didn't correct her. Of course, why would I? It was true."

"Matt, I understand why you'd feel that way. I felt the same way about you. That's why I left the project. But that doesn't have to affect us now."

"But that's not all." He paced. "I instructed Personnel not to give a reference for you at all." His mouth compressed into a thin line. "Ileana pushed me to do it—to hold back a reference—but ultimately it was my decision. I should have been a bigger man, but . . ." He shrugged. At the time, it hadn't seemed anywhere near enough to punish her for her rejection. He knew she was good at what she did, so she'd be okay. He just didn't feel like helping her after the pain she'd caused him.

"But it seems the word got out that you weren't welcome at Cutting Edge Industries, and it's a small tech community, after all."

———

Kate watched the pain etching Matt's features. She could understand why he would refuse giving her a recommendation given the situation. But she remembered how hard it was when her boss told her they were having trouble finding a contract for her, then after a few weeks of her sitting on the bench, how they'd finally laid her off, telling her there wasn't enough work.

"That's why I was let go."

He nodded. "That's not all. When you went looking for work elsewhere, the other consulting companies refused to take you on because your reputation was rapidly crashing. Cutting Edge wouldn't recommend you, your ex-employer had dropped you like a hot potato, and any firms that did come asking about you quickly got the idea they were taking a big chance with their own reputations."

"Are you saying that they were afraid to be associated with me because your company wouldn't have anything to do with me?"

He shrugged. "That's the way it is in business. One black mark can destroy a career."

Pain and anger blazed through Kate. She remembered the panic that had swept through her as weeks, then months passed, and she hadn't been able to get work. At first, her boss had assured her they'd find something, then they had laid her off. She'd approached other consulting firms who had courted her in the past but who now flatly slammed the door in her face. Even the smaller firms. A couple had taken a chance and bid her on a couple of contracts, but those didn't pan out and, finally, one helpful associate had given her the tip about a contract in Connecticut and suggested that starting over in a new location would be a good idea. Everyone had assured her it had been the state of business in New York at the time. She'd had no reason to question it.

But now, to find out that Matt had been the cause of her career plummeting . . .

"You destroyed my career? You ripped away all the good will I'd built up. Wiped out all the hard work I'd put in." Having to pack up and leave everything behind her had been devastating. She'd loved living in New York. She'd had friends. She'd had a great place to live.

She'd had a life she loved. But she'd had to walk away from it all.

"I'm sorry, Kate."

"You're sorry?" She glared at him in amazement. Did he think that could fix everything? "Did you know the effect this was having on me?"

He sighed and stared past her. "I wish I could say I didn't." His gaze caught hers, but at the blaring anger emanating from her, it flicked away. "But I did. I hadn't realized how broad the effect was, but I did know it was causing you problems."

"So you and Ileana must have enjoyed that. The two of you"—she cast a look of disgust at the big bed they'd just shared for their poignant lovemaking—"lying in that bed having a good laugh."

His lips compressed. "I never laughed about it, Kate. I never even discussed it with Ileana. I'd been bitter and angry, and I admit, I wanted to hurt you, but I hated myself for it. Even then. And now. Oh, fuck, what I wouldn't give to take it all back. To make it different."

"But you can't. And you can't change who you are." Her hands clenched into fists and she paced the room. "Why do you think I never wanted to submit to a man? Because you don't care who you hurt. It's all about being in control. Making the world the way *you* want it to be. And if you can't have that, then you strike out to hurt others."

Just like her father had. He'd controlled Kate and he'd controlled her mother. And Matt had done the exact same thing. But she saw it now and she'd never, *ever* let it happen again.

"Kate—"

His tone, the look in his eyes, told her that he was going to make a plea. To proclaim his love again and tell her he was sorry and wanted to make it up to her. But she couldn't take it. She wanted nothing to do with him.

She slashed her hand through the air. "No!" She shoved the sheets away from her, mindless of the fact she stood before him naked, then she strode to the closet, grabbed a pair of jeans and a shirt, and pulled them on, heedless of her lack of underwear. "I'm out of here."

She strode to the door, then retrieved her purse from her room. Moments later, she hurried down the street. She tugged her cell phone from her purse and called for a taxi.

Kate opened the dryer door and pulled out her warm clothes, then placed them in a heap in her blue plastic laundry basket. It had been almost a week since she'd run out on Matt and her heart still clenched at the thought of his betrayal. She dumped the basket of clothes on the sorting table, picked up a light gray shirt, and folded it.

She'd ached knowing how he'd suffered after she'd walked out on him two years ago with no understanding of why it had happened, but then finding out how he'd taken his revenge on her cut her to the core.

"Hey, Kate. There you are."

Kate swung her head around to see Ellen standing in the laundry-room doorway.

"Oh, hi, Ellen."

Kate dropped the folded blouse into the basket, then picked up a striped shirt. She felt a little guilty because she'd been avoiding Ellen, but she knew her friend would pick up on her mood and try to get her to talk about what was wrong. Kate had been nowhere near ready for that.

Ellen grabbed a shirt from Kate's pile and began

folding. "So I thought maybe we'd share a bottle of wine. I have the feeling you could use someone to talk to."

"I don't know. I've got to finish this laundry, then I was going to catch up on some paperwork."

Ellen dropped the folded T-shirt into the basket. "Your laundry's almost done and that paperwork is for the business, right?"

Kate shrugged.

"Business can wait until Monday. Especially since you had booked last week off, yet you came back from your trip early and went into the office anyway." Ellen dropped another T-shirt into the basket. "So? What do you say?"

Kate sighed. Ellen was being a good friend. And Kate could use someone to talk to.

"Okay, but let's make it my place."

Ellen had pictures of her and her boyfriend around her place and the last thing Kate needed was images of a happy couple glowing at her all evening.

Kate sipped her glass of wine as she sat on the couch facing Ellen.

"So, he was the reason you had to move to Connecticut?" Ellen said. "Well, I guess I'll have to thank him."

"Ellen, he ruined my life."

"Really? But you have a business you love, you're your own boss"—she grinned—"and you've got me as a best friend. Is life really so bad?"

Kate's heart ached. "It's true that I've rebuilt my life in spite of what he did. But it doesn't change the fact that he betrayed me. For revenge."

"But think about it, Kate. Would you have been willing to give him a recommendation after what you thought he'd done to you? You said you left the project with his company."

Kate nodded.

"The guy's only human. And I bet he didn't realize what it was doing to your life."

Kate sighed. "I know. I've told myself the same thing. But it was so hard to have to leave everything behind. And it was his fault."

Ellen leaned forward and placed her hand on Kate's. "You know, I don't think this has anything to do with what happened to your job. I think it has to do with the fact that he had control over your life and you think he abused it. I think this has to do with the fact your father was abusive and now you're running scared that Matt will be the same kind of man as your father. But do you think he is?"

"Ellen, when I was a kid, my mom was totally under my dad's control. He controlled what she wore, what money she had to spend, where she went, who she saw. And she let him. I *hated* that. When my aunt took sick and Mom's family called her to come and see Aunt Lily before she died, Dad wouldn't let her go. And the worst was, Mom didn't fight back. Aunt Lily died and Mom was devastated. She didn't get a chance to say good-bye, but she could have, if she hadn't let Dad control her."

"But you're not like that, Kate. You're stronger. You will never let a man control you like that."

Kate shook her head. "How do you know that? I don't know that. When I'm with Matt, I don't know myself. This past week, I had started to believe . . ." A well of emotion flooded her and she sucked in a breath. "I thought that maybe we could make it work. But that was because I trusted him. I knew he would never abuse his control over me. But . . . I mean, now I've seen that, in the right circumstances, he can be selfish and would strike out."

"Oh, Kate, who isn't like that? When we're pushed to the wall, we're all capable of acting out. But think about it. If he'd really been trying to hurt you, he could have done better than that."

"You mean he could have gotten me fired from my job? Oh, wait. He did."

"Okay, I get it. But it wasn't on purpose. He told you he didn't realize the effect his actions were having on you. He simply held back giving you a glowing recommendation. As I said, he's human. I'm sure you wouldn't have been up to telling people what a wonderful human being he was right then, either. On the other hand, if he'd really wanted to hurt you, he could have given you a bad review. He could have said you're unreliable and that your work sucked. That you couldn't be depended on to see a project through, et cetera. If he'd done that, would you even have gotten the job here?"

"I suppose you're right."

"Of course I'm right. Kate, I've seen how you look at that man, and it's clear as day you're in love with him. Right?"

Kate pursed her lips and nodded. "But sometimes love's not enough." Tears welled in her eyes as she remembered how her mother had always said how much she loved her father, yet she'd always seemed so miserable with her life.

"You're only saying that because of your mom and dad, but Kate, Matt isn't the same as your dad. And you're not the same as your mom. You know that deep inside, don't you?"

"Maybe. But that doesn't mean it'll work."

Ellen's eyebrow arched. "Have you thought about the fact that no matter what you decide about being with Matt, you still have to see him on a regular basis because of your business arrangement?"

Had she thought about it? In fact, she'd thought of almost nothing else over the past several days. The big question in her mind was, how could she possibly continue the business arrangement with Matt now?

———

Matt finished the e-mail to his marketing director and hit SEND, then leaned back in his chair and rubbed the back of his neck. He hadn't slept well over the past week, tossing and turning at night with thoughts of Kate. A part of him wanted to go after her and beg her to take him back, while another insisted he seduce her with his authoritative manner and demand she be his.

But, damn it, neither of those approaches would work.

As much as he'd known it had to end between them, that Kate would never love him after finding out what he'd done, it didn't make it any easier.

He glared at his screen, his teeth clenching. He was a man of action. A man who fought for what he wanted.

But he couldn't fight for Kate. He couldn't make Kate love him.

The phone rang and his gaze darted to it. His secretary knew this was the time he blocked off every day to be undisturbed. He snatched up the handset.

"What is it?" he snapped.

"Oh, uh . . . Sorry to disturb you, Mr. Pearce, but . . . I mean, I explained that you don't take visitors right now, but she said it's important. I . . . uh . . . Should I send her away?"

Damn. His secretary was out sick today and now he'd intimidated the hell out of the poor temp.

Why would a woman appear at his door without an appointment? His business associates and senior staff knew he didn't take visitors in the morning. His heart lurched, wondering if it might actually be Kate, but he knew better and tamped down that hope before it could unbalance him. Why would she come all the way here from Connecticut, especially without letting him know? He was sure she wouldn't want to see him, and if she wanted to talk business, she'd probably have her lawyer or one of her staff contact him.

"The woman is quite insistent," the temp said quietly into the phone.

Quite insistent? That sounded more like Ileana.

"Fine, send her in."

He clicked on his browser and opened the calendar window. The door opened and from the corner of his eye as he reviewed his schedule, he caught a quick impression of a woman in a tailored black suit with a pencil-thin skirt, red pumps with stiletto heels, and carrying a red handbag. Definitely Ileana's style.

He had a half hour free before his meeting with the board.

He might as well get this over with because, knowing Ileana, whatever it was she wanted, she wouldn't let it slide. He leaned back in his chair.

"So, Ileana, what is it you want?"

But the woman standing before him was not Ileana. He sucked in a breath and stared at her, ensuring that he wasn't seeing things.

"Kate?"

"You were expecting Ileana?" She closed the door behind her and glanced around his office.

"No, of course not. It's just that when my secretary . . . the temp . . . said a woman was insisting to see me . . ." He stood up. "I don't take visitors this time of day."

"Yes, she made that clear. So I'm disturbing you."

"No, Kate. Not at all. Please come in and sit down." He gestured to the chair facing his desk.

She stepped farther into his big office, but paused yards from his desk. She stood tall and confident, commanding the room. Her presence surrounded him, mesmerizing him.

Silence hung between them as he waited for her to say something, but finally he needed to break the silence. "Why are you here, Kate?"

"You and I have unfinished business to discuss."

"I have a meeting in a half hour," he stated distractedly, concerned it didn't give them much time, but he instantly regretted saying it aloud.

"All right, another time then." She turned and headed toward the door.

"No, wait. I can cancel." He snatched up the phone, relieved to see Kate stop and turn back. He did not want her to leave. The temp picked up. "Cancel my next meeting, and I'm not to be disturbed."

He hung up. "I'm all yours, Kate." Body and soul. If only she wanted him.

She frowned. "What I want to discuss is sensitive. I don't want anyone walking in."

"My secretary won't let anyone in."

She raised an eyebrow. "And yet, she let me in even though she had standing instructions not to allow anyone to disturb you."

He sighed and nodded. "Point taken. I'll lock the door."

Damn. That meant this was going to get messy.

When he'd told her what he'd done, she hadn't yelled or screamed, or even cried. She'd just walked out. Clearly, she'd chosen now to let him know what she thought of him, and she didn't want anyone walking in on their emotional confrontation.

He strode across the office and locked the door, then he turned back to face her.

"So why are you here, Kate?"

"If I told you I'm not comfortable with you having any control whatsoever of my company, would you be willing to dissolve the business agreement between us?"

His chest tightened. "That's not a good idea." They both knew that without the capital he was providing, her company would fail.

She walked to the round table by the window where he held one-on-one meetings and placed her slim leather briefcase on the tabletop, then opened it and pulled out a document.

"I've had my lawyer draw up papers to replace our business agreement. Essentially, to dissolve the partnership. I'd like you to sign it."

"Do you have another investor?"

If she didn't, her business would not survive and he hated the thought that she would let it die, just to cut the connection between them completely.

"No, but I do have something I hope will pan out."

She held out the document and he stepped forward and took it from her hand. He caught a whiff of her lilac shampoo, a new scent for her. Delicate and enticing.

He glanced over the typewritten words, most blurring under his quick perusal, but it was clear what it was. Kate was cutting him loose.

He glanced up from the paper and met her gaze. "Are you sure you want to do this, Kate?"

"Under the circumstances, the agreement no longer works as is, so yes, I'm sure."

He sighed and pulled a pen from the inner pocket of his jacket, then set the agreement on the table and signed. Then he handed it to her.

"Is there anything else, Kate?"

"Yes, we haven't even begun to deal with the fact that you nearly destroyed my whole career."

He nodded, his heart aching. "I know. If there was

any way I could make it up to you, I would, but I know there's nothing I can do to offset the pain I caused you."

"Actually, there is something."

Kate almost laughed at the way his gaze shot up to hers, then at the perplexed expression on his face.

"What is it?" he asked.

"Well, you caused me pain, so I should cause you pain."

She placed the signed agreement beside her briefcase on the table, then opened the case again and reached into the leather divider in the lid. Her fingers found the pencil-thin crop and she pulled it out, then turned to face him.

"You should be punished for what you did."

His gaze darted to the leather-wrapped riding crop with the rhinestone-trimmed handle and the heart-shaped leather tag on the end. His expression didn't change, but she could see the gleam in his eyes.

"You want to punish me?"

She resisted letting her lips turn up in a smile. "That's right. Now, stand facing your desk and take off your jacket."

He walked to his desk and turned his back to her, then slipped off his jacket and tossed it onto his leather chair behind the desk.

"Now, drop your pants."

She watched as the belt loosened, then the pants slipped to the floor and landed with a clunk. He stepped out of them and kicked them aside. He now stood in his shirt and boxers, but she needed to see bare ass.

"Now, the boxers."

"Yes, Mistress."

She couldn't prevent the smile this time. Her heartbeat increased as his boxers dropped, but his shirt covered his fine ass.

"Pull your shirt out of the way." She drew in a deep breath as he revealed his tight, hard buttocks. "Very good, now bend over."

She stepped toward him as he obeyed, bracing himself against the desk. Then she flicked the crop back and slashed through the air until it connected with his gorgeous ass. A red mark appeared, in the shape of a heart. That's why she'd chosen this crop. Because she liked the idea of leaving red hearts on his ass.

She flicked the crop again, on the other cheek this time, then watched the heart appear.

"Does that hurt?" she asked.

"Yes, Mistress."

A part of her told her to stop.

"Do you want me to do it again?"

"Yes, Mistress." This time his words came out in a sexy rumble.

God, this was turning him on, too.

She smacked again, forming another heart. Then again.

She stepped back and admired her handiwork.

"Please punish me, Mistress. I was very bad."

"I will punish you." She stepped closer and ran her fingertips over the angry red flesh, needing to touch him. His skin was hot where it was red. She glided her fingertip around one heart, then she stroked his hard, muscular butt with her palm. "Now, turn around."

She stepped back as he straightened up. When he turned around, her gaze shot straight to his rock-hard cock, the fabric of his shirt draping over it.

Oh, God, she wanted to touch it. To feel it in her hand.

"Go sit in your chair." Her voice came out raspy so she cleared her throat.

She walked to her briefcase again and retrieved the black leather bands she'd brought. He sat in the black executive chair now and she approached him, her gaze falling again to his big cock, which was standing straight up. Long and hard.

"Put your hands on the armrests."

When he complied, she wrapped one of the leather bands around his wrist, binding it to the armrest, then fastened it. She then bound his other wrist in the same way.

She smiled at the sight of him sitting there, helpless

before her. She leaned forward and stroked the tip of his hard cock and watched him twitch.

She stepped back and leaned against the desk.

"Now, maybe I should go let that secretary of yours in here. I wonder if she'd be shocked seeing you like this." She grinned. "Or maybe she'd climb aboard and give you the ride of your life." She glanced toward the door. "That could be fun to watch."

She could tell Matt wasn't worried in the least. He knew she'd be more embarrassed than he was if the woman walked in here right now. He also knew she'd never share him.

"Yes, Mistress. That would be a severe punishment. Having that beautiful young woman climb on top of me and ride me to orgasm. My hard cock gliding in and out of her. Her wet pussy clenching around me."

Oh, God, he knew what he was doing. Her insides melted and she longed for that hot, hard cock of his to be inside her right now.

"No, I think I can find other ways to torture you."

She unbuttoned her suit jacket and his gaze locked onto her chest as the garment opened, revealing her red bra beneath. It was trimmed with delicate black lace, but the cups were made of totally transparent red fabric, so he could clearly see her breasts and the hard nipples. She stroked a finger over one bud. Her insides quivered. She stroked the other, seeing his blue eyes darken as he watched. She pushed herself from the desk and reached behind her to unfasten the skirt, then she shimmied it downward until it fell to the floor. She wore equally transparent panties. His gaze shifted to her crotch. She stroked her hand over her stomach, then lower. As her fingers glided under the fabric, his breath caught. She pushed her fingers into her folds, then inside her damp opening. She was so hot, and anxious to have his big cock inside her. She ripped off her panties, then turned and leaned over the desk.

"Lick me," she demanded.

"Yes, Mistress."

He might be bound to the chair, but she knew that wouldn't stop him. He rolled the chair forward until it pressed against the backs of her legs, his legs on either side of hers, then he leaned forward. She felt his slightly whisker-roughened cheek brush her upper thigh. She grasped her ass and opened to reveal her wet folds to him, then almost jumped as she felt his tongue brush against her.

He licked the length of her slit several times, then he pushed his tongue into her opening and wiggled, sending heat through her. He shifted and his tongue found her clit. He flicked against it, but couldn't quite reach as well as she'd like.

She could release his hands so he could maneuver better, but she didn't want to do that yet.

"Stop."

His face moved away and she turned around as best she could with the chair against her. He leaned forward and his tongue found her clit again and flicked.

"Oh." Pleasure vibrated through her.

He flicked again, then drove his tongue into her.

She placed her hands on the front of the armrests and pushed the chair backward, giving her space. Dropping to her knees, she wrapped her hands around his hard shaft, then licked him. He groaned as she wrapped her mouth around him, and swirled her tongue over him. Then she glided down, taking him deep inside her throat.

"Oh, God, that feels good."

She drew back, then took him deep again. He arched his pelvis as she squeezed him.

She dropped him from her mouth, then climbed onto his lap, resting her knees on either side of his legs. If she released his hands, he could stroke her breasts and pull her tight to him, his hands cupping her ass, but she liked having this control over him. She cupped her breast and leaned forward, pressing her nipple to his mouth. His tongue darted out and he licked her, his raspy tongue dragging over her sensitive nub. Then he took it in his

mouth and sucked. She moaned at the exquisite sensation. She pressed her other breast to his mouth and he
licked her nipple, then sucked it, too.

"Oh, God, I want you." She leaned back and ripped
open his shirt, sending buttons scattering. She licked his
hard chest, then grazed his hard nipple with her teeth,
eliciting a groan.

She wrapped her hand around his thick cock, then
pressed it to her opening. His big cockhead stroked her
wet flesh as she rocked his cock back and forth, then she
positioned him and glided downward, taking his hard
flesh deep inside.

He groaned and jerked his pelvis up, driving deeper.
She gasped, then squeezed him inside her.

She leaned close to his neck and nuzzled, then murmured, "I'm in control now, do you understand? Dis-
please me and I'll leave you aching and wanting. Please
me and I'll give you the satisfaction you need."

His head dropped back against the chair. "Yes, Mistress, I'm yours to command."

She smiled and lifted herself, reveling in the feel of
his big cockhead dragging along her passage, then she
glided down. Slowly. She glided up and down again.
His body stiffened as she took him deep, again and again.
She moved faster, his shaft filling her. She squeezed it, so
hard and thick.

Pleasure swamped her senses and she moaned.

"Oh, God, yeah." Matt's voice was deep and hoarse.

She kissed his neck. "Call me 'Mistress.'"

"Yes, Mistress. It feels so good."

Her breathing was fast and heat enveloped her. "Tell me more."

"My cock is aching inside you. You feel so good around me that it hurts. It's going to explode any minute now."

She gazed at his face. "Not yet. Not until I say so." She squeezed him and he groaned. It was so sexy commanding him to pleasure her.

His body was tense and his face contorted in delicious agony. She smiled and drew out the moment, continuing to squeeze him in her hot passage, her own pleasure rising as he quivered with need.

"Please, Mistress," he murmured.

She was barely able to hold back her own orgasm, but she feigned a moment of consideration before she nodded. "You may come now."

He shuddered and she felt hot liquid fill her insides. She glided her finger between them and flicked her clit. Wild sensations fluttered through her and she moaned as an exquisite orgasm erupted inside her.

She groaned as she continued to ride him, his big cock still stretching her as she bounced up and down, the wave of pleasure pulsing through her. Finally, she

collapsed against him, mild eddies of pleasure still washing through her.

She could hear his heartbeat against her ear as she
clung to his broad shoulders. She pushed herself to her
knees, letting his spent cock slip from her, then she
stood up.

"Is it clear now who is in charge?" she asked with a
wicked grin.

He smiled. "You are, Mistress." He gazed up at her,
then his expression turned serious. "You have always
been in charge."

She drew in a breath. He'd said that kind of thing
before, but she realized she was now beginning to believe him. And that gave her confidence.

She unfastened his wrists and tossed the leather straps
on the desk.

"What would you like me to do for you now, Mistress?"

She smiled. "Well, there is one thing." She walked
toward the table and turned to face him again. "Come
over here and kneel in front of me."

He stood up and approached her, looming over her
as he drew near, but then he knelt in front of her.

"Now, what do you think you should do while on
your knees in front of me?"

He gazed up at her, then rested his hand on her
stomach and stroked downward as he leaned forward.

She ran her fingers through his hair and grabbed a handful, then drew his head back.

"No, not that. Think really hard. What did you tell me you were going to get on your knees for two years ago?"

His eyes lit up. "Really, Kate?"

She arched a mischievous eyebrow. "What happened to calling me 'Mistress'?"

He smiled. "Yes, Mistress." He took her hand in his and raised it to his mouth, then kissed it. "Mistress, I love you with all my heart. I want you in my life always and will dedicate my life to making you happy. Will you marry me?"

Despite the fact they were both practically naked, and Matt had called her 'Mistress,' and they were acting out a crazy, funny sex fantasy . . . tears brimmed in her eyes. Because she had never been happier.

She nodded, then found her voice and said, "Yes, Matt. I'll marry you."

He bounded to his feet and pulled her into his arms. The passion of his mouth on hers swept her away. Their tongues danced and her heart pounded.

"Oh, God, Kate, I love you so much."

"And I love you, Matt. I have always loved you."

He caressed her cheek. "And you know, sweetheart, that I will never control you. Or your company."

She smiled. "I know that. I knew having you sign

the termination agreement didn't matter because when we get married, we will be equal owners anyway."

He smiled and tipped up her chin. "You really were punishing me."

"Well, I had to ensure you were truly contrite. And that you would follow instructions when push came to shove."

He laughed. "I will always follow your instructions, my love." He kissed her again, leaving her breathless. "And you realize that you will also own half of my business. And since I am ultimately under your control—because I would never say no to you—you are now in charge of a very big corporation."

The magnitude of what he said hit her. She didn't know how to run a company the size of Matt's. She drew in a deep breath.

"You'll handle whatever I tell you to, though, right?"

He chuckled. "Of course, my love. I'll do anything you tell me to do."

"Good. So, right now, I'm feeling very turned on by all the power at my disposal." She flattened her hand on his chest and dragged it down his muscular flesh, heading for his delightfully rising cock. "So, right now, I'd like you to be my Master and have your way with me." She wrapped her hand around his hard shaft and squeezed.

He grinned. "Until you say otherwise?"

"That's right." She stepped back, knowing this marriage was going to be a roller coaster of wild times, and crazy power plays. But, ultimately, she knew that Matt would always defer to her desires.

She smiled. "So what would you like me to do, Sir?"

Epilogue

Matt opened the front door and stepped into the house.

"Kate," he called as he set his suitcases on the floor. His driver had offered to bring them in, but Matt had declined. After three weeks away, he didn't want the driver's presence, no matter how brief, to interfere with a warm reception from Kate.

"Matt?" Kate burst into the hallway and rushed toward him.

He was home a day early. She flung herself into his arms and their mouths met with hungry passion. She unfastened the three buttons of his cashmere coat and pushed it and his suit jacket underneath from his shoulders, then down until they fell to the floor, while her tongue glided past his lips, aggressively exploring the inside of his mouth.

He drew back with a laugh. "Hey, at least let me close the door."

He pushed the door closed, then kicked off his shoes. As soon as he stood up, she wrapped her arms around his neck and pulled him back to continue their kiss.

"I'm glad you're back." The tone of her voice sounded serious and he glanced into her glittering blue eyes. She seemed on the verge of tears.

"Kate, is there something wrong?"

She shook her head. "No, I've just missed you so much."

He tightened his grip on her. "Oh, me, too, baby." He captured her lips again, enjoying her almost desperate response to his kisses.

"And I'm so turned on." Her fingers played down the front of his shirt, releasing buttons along the way, then one hand glided inside and pinched his nipple, sending sharp twangs of pleasure through him.

"God, so am I." He had been aching for her the whole time he'd been gone. Her other hand stroked over his swelling cock and he groaned. He grasped her wrists and guided her back a step.

"All right, slave. Time for you to do what I say."

She stepped back another step and smiled. "Yes, Master."

This was new. She hadn't called him Master before.

She smiled impishly and drew in a deep breath, thrusting her bosom up high, then slowly released it. "May I call you Master, Sir?"

"Yes, I like that." And he really did. His cock twitched at thoughts of her murmuring the term of respect into his ear as he pushed his cock inside her, then later her begging him, as her master, to fuck her deeply.

"Now, take off your blouse."

"Yes, Master." Her fingers moved down the front of her blouse, releasing buttons. She fumbled on one and, clearly impatient, she tore the sides of the blouse apart, scattering the last few buttons to the floor. They bounced across the hardwood floor as she dropped the blouse from her shoulders and tossed it across the oak banister behind her.

He couldn't pull his gaze from the creamy swell of her breasts rising and falling, the soft mounds lifted by a coffee-colored bra trimmed with cream lace.

He watched in fascination as she stroked her breasts. He could see the nipples tenting the delicate lace, and his breath caught as her fingertips glided over one.

"Now, the skirt." Would her undies match the delightful bra?

She dropped her pencil-thin skirt to the floor and stepped out of it.

Of course they matched. Kate loved matching sets. And she wore coffee-colored stockings, the kind that stayed up without garters.

Her fingers glided down her hip, then stroked along the milky thigh above her stockings, moving toward the inner thigh. His cock swelled painfully at the sight. If he didn't stop her, would she slide under the crotch of her panties and stroke her soft folds? Were they wet already with wanting him?

If she did, he was pretty sure he'd blow his load right here while watching her.

"Kate, come here and show me how much you missed me."

He stroked the bulge in his pants, giving her a clear indication of what he wanted. She grinned and approached, then dropped to her knees in front of him. Her fingers moving on his zipper sent his cock twitching. Then her warm hand wrapped around his shaft and he groaned in delight.

"May I suck your big cock, Master?"

Oh, fuck, yeah.

"Yes, slave," he said with as calm a voice as he could. When her lips wrapped around him, she took him deep into her mouth, and he thought he'd die from the euphoric sensation.

She took him deeper, then glided back, then deeper again, driving his pleasure higher. He was so fucking close.

"Stop." The word came out sharper than he'd intended, but she drew back with a smile on her face.

She stood up and reached behind her, then unfastened her bra. She pulled it away, revealing her big, swollen nipples. Bigger than life, it seemed in his feverish need. He leaned down and licked one, then sucked it deep. She moaned and arched toward him, pushing deeper into his mouth.

He moved to the other nipple and she cried out, hugging his head tight to her bosom, her fingers coiling through his hair.

When he released her, he stared at her flushed cheeks and the desire glittering in her eyes. She seemed almost desperate for him. He smiled broadly. Well, why the hell not? He was desperate for her.

As if she couldn't stand being under his scrutiny a second longer, she spun around and walked to the banister. She slipped off her panties, and then without a word leaned forward and spread her legs wide.

He'd looked forward to getting home and having a long, romantic evening with her, to be the loving husband and woo her with wine and music and soft words of love, but he realized now that had been completely unrealistic. They had been apart too long and both of them were too horny.

He stepped toward her, shedding his pants as he went. When he was behind her, he dropped his boxers to the floor. Now he was standing in only his shirt, tie, and socks behind his beautiful, naked wife, who was hungry for him to fuck her. Life didn't get better than this.

There would be time later for their romantic evening. He wrapped his hand around his cock and pressed it to her ass, loving the needy murmurs she made. He pushed between her thighs, gliding over her wet flesh. Oh, fuck, she was wet.

"Please, Master, don't torture me." Her words sounded almost tearful with desire. "I need you inside me."

"Oh, God, baby. What you're doing to me . . ." He pressed the tip of his cock to her opening, then drove in deep.

She gasped, clinging to the wooden banister as she pushed her ass tight against him.

He drew back and drove deep again. Then again. Her breathing accelerated as he thrust into her, his own pleasure building with each stroke.

"Oh, God, oh, God, oh, God." Then she wailed, louder and louder as his cock plunged into her repeatedly.

His tight balls seemed to explode and he erupted inside her with a groan.

And still she wailed, riding the wave of their shared ecstasy.

Finally, she quieted, then slumped against the railing. He leaned against her back, his arms wrapping snugly against her waist, holding her to him.

He tucked his arm under her knees, lifted her, and

carried her up the stairs and into their room. He laid her gently on the bed and stepped back and unfastened the rest of his shirt buttons, then pulled off his tie. As he slipped free of the rest of his clothes, to his surprise, Kate pushed herself up and sat on the side of the bed. He thought she was sated for now and was ready for some cuddle time, but she seemed to have something else in mind.

"Master, I'm sorry I overstepped my bounds downstairs before you instructed me. Do you wish to punish me?"

"Uh . . . yes, I do. Go and get the flogger."

Kate, still totally naked, went to the cupboard and reached inside. Then, to his surprise, she walked toward him with the blue suede flogger. The pink one he'd introduced her to in the dungeon was the one they used, because with its wide, soft suede tails, he used it more to massage her skin than to cause pain, though if he flicked it just right, it could sting a little. The blue one had thinner tails and could cause a more painful sting.

She handed it to him and then walked to the bed, tossed some pillows in front of her, and leaned over. Her lower torso rested on the pillows while she thrust her ass up into the air. He stepped behind her and rested the tails of the flogger on her back, so that she could get used to the feel of it, then he dragged the tails slowly across her skin, stroking her back and ass, then along her inner thighs. He dragged the flogger back up, still stroking lightly.

She wiggled her ass as if trying to get his attention, which worked perfectly. He stared at her perfect round cheeks as the blue suede strips glided over them.

"God damn it, punish me." Her words crackled with annoyance, startling him.

"Kate?"

"I mean, please, Master. I'm sorry I disobeyed you. I *need* to be punished."

He'd never seen Kate so . . . so . . . he wasn't sure how to describe it, but it was different.

He dragged the flogger over her one more time, then flicked it back and cracked it over her ass.

"Oh, yes!"

From the sound, that must have smarted, and he could see her skin flush. He flicked again, and she moaned. Her skin turned deeper red, and he stroked his hand over it soothingly, but she wiggled again.

"More. Harder," she said breathlessly.

God, what had gotten into her? He flicked once more, but he also stroked his hand between her thighs, wanting to distract her from the flogger. If he continued at this pace, angry welts would appear on her ass. He didn't want to hurt her, even if that's what she seemed to want right now.

He kept whipping her ass, but with light, pleasurable

strokes now, while his fingers glided along her wet folds, then slipped inside her.

"I want you to fuck my ass." She pushed her butt higher in the air. "But I also want you in my pussy."

His ears perked up in surprise. Kate never said the word "pussy."

"Lie still, slave." He patted her ass lightly, pressing her down against the cushions. He walked to the cupboard and returned with a vibrator. He'd picked one that was shaped like a natural cock, but wasn't as big as his. He pressed it to her pussy and slid it inside her. She murmured softly as he swirled it inside her, then he drew it out and pressed it to the little puckered opening of her ass.

Her ass arched upward eagerly.

"Relax." He pushed forward and slid it into her back opening.

"Oh, yes. Oh, that feels so good." Her words had the edge of desperate pleasure.

Once it was fully inside, he sat down on the bed beside her, keeping his hand on the vibrator so it would stay in place. "Come over here."

She pushed herself to her feet and slipped onto his lap, her knees resting on the bed on either side of him. He pressed his aching cock to her pussy and glided inside.

"Now, fuck me, slave."

"Oh, yes, Master." She raised her body up, then glided down on him. Then again. Her sweet, smooth passage cocooned him in delicious heat as she took him in and out, over and over.

He gripped her hip with one hand, still holding the vibrator in the other. He flicked it on, and as it started to vibrate inside her ass, she groaned, then moved on him faster. Within moments she took him deep and arched her back, wailing in another orgasm. He jerked inside her, his cock exploding as he reached his own climax at the sight of her in ecstasy.

A few minutes later, as he held her close to him in bed, the darkness surrounding them, he noticed that Kate was breathing deeply, and a bit erratically. He stroked her hair back behind her ear and felt dampness on her cheek.

What the fuck?

"Kate, what's wrong?"

"Nothing, I . . ." She sucked in a deep breath, then snuggled closer. "I'm just really happy to have you home."

In the morning, he still wondered at her tears, but she assured him nothing was wrong. Still, she seemed tense, and to both their surprise, she even snapped at him once, which was highly unusual for Kate.

When they sat down to breakfast, he watched her over the table. "Kate, I really wish you'd tell me what's wrong."

Anger flared in her eyes. "I told you nothing's wrong."

He raised an eyebrow, not letting her mood intimidate him. "Really?" He smiled, hoping to keep the mood light. "Somehow I'm not convinced."

Her hands rolled into fists and she pushed herself from the table and paced. "Really. I'm just . . . I don't know . . . out of sorts." She walked to the counter and pulled a mug from the cupboard.

"You have a cup of coffee here, Kate."

She glanced around as she filled the cup with water and put it into the microwave. "I know. But I feel like herbal tea instead."

As Kate waited for the microwave to boil the water, her cell phone chimed. Matt picked it up from the table and held it out to her, but not before seeing "Medical Center" on the display. She took the phone and answered it as she returned to the microwave to fetch her cup and set it on the counter.

"Yes. Hi, yeah." She glanced at Matt and then turned away, grabbing a box of tea bags as she listened on the phone.

"But how could that happen? I'm so careful." She nodded. "Okay. I understand. Yes, I'll come into the office tomorrow." She dropped a tea bag into the cup and stirred absently, spilling water on the counter. "What? No, I'm not alone. Matt came home early. Okay."

She set her cell on the counter, heedless of how close it was to the spilled water, totally unlike her usual careful self.

"Kate, what is it?"

"That was Ellen."

"Kate, I saw that it was from a medical center."

Kate nodded, her back still to him. "That's right. Ellen is a nurse. My doctor is in the office where she works. Ellen recommended her when I first got to town."

"So why is she calling you?"

Kate still hadn't turned around and it was making him nervous.

"For the past few weeks I've been feeling . . . weird. I thought it was because I was missing you. I've been irritable and cranky and . . . well, horny in the extreme. Ellen suggested I see the doctor earlier this week and they did some tests."

His stomach plummeted. "And? Was Ellen calling with the results?"

Kate nodded as she turned to him. When he saw the tears streaming from her eyes, his stomach lurched. He surged to his feet and toward her. "Good God, Kate, what did they find?"

The tears streamed more freely now and she wiped them away, her lip trembling.

"Oh, God, Matt. I don't know what to do. I don't want you to leave me."

"Leave you? What the hell are you talking about?" He wiped the tears from her eyes and looked at her imploringly. "Kate, just tell me what they found."

"I'm . . ." She sucked in a breath and gazed up at him. "I'm pregnant."

He froze, sure he'd heard her wrong. "You're what?"

"I'm pregnant." Then more tears flooded from her eyes.

"Pregnant, as in, you're going to be a mother?"

She nodded.

"Kate, don't you want to have a baby?"

She nodded some more. "More than anything."

He sucked in a breath. "Okay, then, isn't that good?"

"No, because you don't want a baby."

"I don't?"

She gazed up at him with wide eyes. "Do you?"

Confusion swirled through him and combined with the fear that she was dreadfully ill, the elation that she was with child, which he couldn't quite allow to surface, and the complete lack of understanding at her reaction.

He waved his hands back and forth. "Okay, let's just focus for a minute. You're going to have a baby," he said in wonder.

She nodded and his mouth turned up in an almost painful grin as he released his fear of something being wrong and allowed the good news to seep in. "And I'm going to be a father."

She nodded again.

"Oh, Matt, I know you didn't want to have a baby,

but the doctor said this can happen sometimes. Even on birth control."

He took her hands. "Kate, whatever gave you the idea that I didn't want to have a baby?"

She pursed her lips. "When you forgot to wear a condom that time—before you knew I was on birth control. You said you didn't want a pregnancy to be the result. It seemed really important to you."

He laughed and pulled her in for a big kiss. "No, Kate, that was just because I didn't believe we could be together, even though I desperately wanted us to be." He stroked her hair back from her face. "And you know how much I want you. I just didn't want to put you through that . . . having a baby with a man you didn't love. Who wasn't, and could never be, your husband." His smile broadened. "But all that changed."

He kissed her again, then gazed deeply into her shimmering eyes. "I love you so much. And having a baby with you is one of the biggest joys I could ever experience."

Her eyes filled with tears again. "Oh, Matt. I love you so much."

She wrapped her arms around him and kissed him. Her soft lips moved sweetly on his.

As he held her, their bodies pressed tightly together, her loving kiss turned more passionate, and she plunged her tongue deep into his mouth and swirled.

"Oh, God, Matt. I'm so turned on." She began tugging on his robe, then pulling it open.

His cock swelled at the feel of her hands stroking over his chest, then tweaking his nipples.

God, he could tell this was going to be a long, chaotic pregnancy.

And he was going to enjoy every second of it.

Fulfill all your wildest fantasies with Opal Carew...

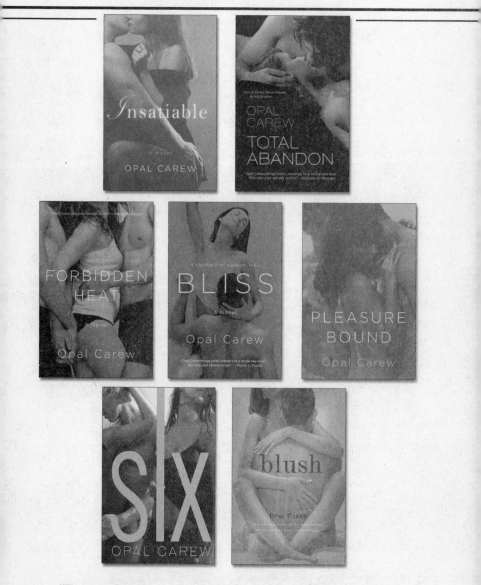

"Beautiful erotic romance...real and powerful."
—*RT Book Reviews*

 St. Martin's Griffin